"I want to go out with you."

Eric smiled as he made his announcement.

A tiny, perfect V creased Alina's forehead as she studied him. "You know I have to return to Croatia in the middle of January."

The reminder sent a stab of pain through his chest. "We've got almost three months until then."

"So…we go out for three months, and then I leave?"

Did she have to state things so bluntly? He much preferred to pretend January would never get here. "We could have a lot of fun in that time," he said. "You could go home with some good memories."

"You're promising me good memories?" Her eyes sparkled with amusement, teasing him.

He leaned closer, and put his hand at her waist. "We could make some very good memories," he whispered.

Dear Reader,

I think Christmas is the most romantic time of year—more romantic, even, than Valentine's Day. After all, the whole idea behind Christmas is love, and this has translated into acts such as gift giving, and getting together with family and friends. As well as acts of charity and thinking of those less fortunate.

Christmas is so romantic to me that I was married at Christmastime. Instead of orange blossoms and roses, the church was decorated with evergreens, poinsettia and a Christmas tree. My husband and I celebrate our anniversary only a few days before Christmas each year, and the festive atmosphere only adds to our joy.

So when I was given the opportunity to write a Christmas romance, I was thrilled. Crested Butte, Colorado, with its small-town charm, snow and multiple Christmas trees, seemed the perfect romantic setting for this story. Alina and Eric come from different backgrounds and even different countries, but they've both found a home in Colorado. As they learn about each other's holiday customs, they see how their differences can add variety and interest to their relationship and how the love they share can bring them together.

I hope you enjoy reading their story. I love to hear from readers. Write to me at Cindi@CindiMyers.com or in care of Harlequin Enterprises Ltd., 225 Duncan Mill Road, Don Mills, ON M3B 3K9, Canada.

Happy reading,

Cindi Myers

Her Christmas Wish
CINDI MYERS

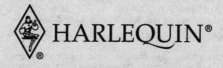

HARLEQUIN®

TORONTO • NEW YORK • LONDON
AMSTERDAM • PARIS • SYDNEY • HAMBURG
STOCKHOLM • ATHENS • TOKYO • MILAN • MADRID
PRAGUE • WARSAW • BUDAPEST • AUCKLAND

Recycling programs
for this product may
not exist in your area.

ISBN-13: 978-0-373-75291-1

HER CHRISTMAS WISH

Copyright © 2009 by Cynthia Myers.

Printed in U.S.A.

ABOUT THE AUTHOR

Cindi Myers's favorite holiday is Christmas. She loves the decorations, the gifts and especially the food. Her idea of a romantic evening is sipping spiked eggnog, eating Christmas cookies and sitting with her honey admiring the lit Christmas tree while snow falls outside. Christmas carols are optional, but there should definitely be mistletoe.

Books by Cindi Myers

HARLEQUIN AMERICAN ROMANCE
1182—MARRIAGE ON HER MIND
1199—THE RIGHT MR. WRONG
1259—THE MAN MOST LIKELY
1268—THE DADDY AUDITION

HARLEQUIN SUPERROMANCE
1498—A SOLDIER COMES HOME
1530—A MAN TO RELY ON
1549—CHILD'S PLAY

HARLEQUIN NEXT
MY BACKWARDS LIFE
THE BIRDMAN'S DAUGHTER

HARLEQUIN SIGNATURE SELECT
LEARNING CURVES
BOOTCAMP
  "Flirting with an Old Flame"

HARLEQUIN ANTHOLOGY
A WEDDING IN PARIS
  "Picture Perfect"

For Muna

Chapter One

"Don't look now, but there's a really hot guy watching you."

"Oh?" Alina Allinova started to turn and scan the crowd gathered for the culmination of Crested Butte's Vinotok fall festival.

Her friend Marissa Alvarez put a hand on her shoulder to stop her. "Don't look. He's staring right at us." She giggled. "Really, he can't take his eyes off you. It's like he's in love with you."

Alina's stomach fluttered. The idea of a handsome stranger falling instantly in love with her was preposterous, but wonderfully romantic and exciting. The kind of thing she'd fantasized about, though she'd never admit it out loud. "If you won't let me look at him, at least tell me what he looks like," she said. "Is he blond?"

"No, not blond. His hair is brown."

"Oh." Not that it really mattered… "Maybe it's that dark blond that looks brown in a certain light. Is he a big guy?"

Marissa shook her head. "Not that big. And his hair is a very dark brown, almost black."

Alina turned all the way around and caught the eye of the stranger.

Her heart sped up again. Okay, he was good-looking. Dark brown hair fell across his forehead, above a pair of eyes the color of roasted coffee beans that seemed to stare right through her. When their gazes met, he smiled, revealing perfect white teeth against his olive skin.

"Girl, how are you even standing here with a man watching you like that?" Marissa whispered. "I'd be melting right into the ground if a gorgeous guy ever looked at me that way."

The man took a step toward them. Alina immediately whirled around, embarrassed to be caught staring.

Marissa grabbed her arm. "Why are you turning away? Hello? The man is hot."

Alina didn't have time to explain. Mr. Gorgeous was by her side. "Hi, I'm Eric Sepulveda," he said, offering his hand.

Alina went wobbly in the knees when he took her hand, and immediately felt ridiculous. "Alina Allinova," she said, and withdrew her fingers from his, though the warmth of his touch lingered on her skin.

"Where are you from, Alina?" he asked. "Not from around here, I'm guessing."

That smile again, which sent her stomach fluttering wildly. *Get a grip, girl.* "I'm from Gunnison," she said. She said it merely to be contrary—she knew that wasn't what he'd meant. Her accent gave her away as a foreigner as soon as she opened her mouth, though people couldn't always place her country of origin.

"Are you a student at the college?" he asked.

"No, I'm a respiratory therapist at Gunnison Valley Hospital."

"Then I can't believe I haven't see you before. I'm over there all the time."

She arched one eyebrow. "What brings you to the hospital so much?" Did he have an ill family member? *He* certainly looked healthy enough. He wasn't that tall—maybe five ten or so—but he had muscular shoulders and a slim waist.

He laughed, a completely masculine sound that served only to stoke the fire of her libido. "No, I'm a paramedic," he said. "We make fairly regular runs to GVH."

"I work on the floor." She was occasionally called upon to treat a patient in the E.R., but she'd never run into Eric before. She wouldn't have forgotten him if she had.

The crowd surged around them, forcing them closer together. Someone behind her bumped into her and Eric put out his hand to steady her. She couldn't stop herself from leaning into him, aware of the strength and warmth in his grip, catching a whiff of the subtle spice of his cologne. What in the world was happening to her? She hadn't even had anything to drink tonight, yet she felt giddy and a little out of control.

"Where are you from before you came to Gunnison?" Eric asked.

"Croatia. In Maksimer, part of the capital, Zagreb." She savored the names on her tongue, the familiar sounds of home that she didn't have the chance to say too often.

"I hear Croatia's a beautiful country," he said.

At least he hadn't asked if all the girls in Croatia were as beautiful as her, or said there must be something in the water there or some similar line, all of which she'd heard multiple times from college students, ski bums and various local Lotharios. The women in her family were generally considered beauties, so she'd dealt with her fair share of attention all her life. As a result, she appreciated a little originality from any man who was interested in her.

Trying not to stare, she checked his hair again. No way he'd ever been close to blond.

The crowd roared with laughter, and Alina turned to see one of the characters in the closing play—some guy in pink tights and doublet—in the throes of an overly dramatic death scene while a man in a dragon suit nearby did a jig.

"Have you been to Vinotok before?" Eric asked, his mouth very close to her ear.

"No," she answered, eyes still focused on the players, though every part of her was aware of the man standing so close. "I read in the paper that this was based on an old Yugoslavian wine festival, so I wanted to see if anything about it was familiar." At his puzzled look, she hastened to explain, "Croatia used to be part of Yugoslavia."

Eric glanced at the actors. A woman with a dozen or so small children gathered about her was speaking. "Do they do this kind of thing in Croatia?" he asked.

Alina laughed. "No. We have a lot of local celebrations in my country, but nothing like this." A man dressed entirely in green, his skin painted green, as well, joined the woman with all the children.

"Crested Butte is kind of known for originality when it comes to holidays," Eric said.

Alina nodded. In the eight months she'd lived in Gunnison, Colorado, she and friends had made numerous trips to the smaller mountain town to ski, hike, bike or enjoy the shops and restaurants on the picturesque main street. The people were friendly, the scenery beautiful and there was always something to do and see.

A collective sigh rose from the crowd, and Alina stood on tiptoe, attempting to see what all the fuss was about. The man in green was kneeling before the woman, who stared at him, a stunned look on her face.

"Isn't that romantic?" Marissa said. "He's proposing!"

"I bet that's a first for Vinotok," Eric said.

The woman pulled the man to his feet and kissed him. The crowd roared and cheered, and behind the happy couple a large papier-mâché figure burst into flame.

"What is that?" Alina asked.

"That's the Grump," Eric said. "For the past couple of weeks there have been boxes in stores and restaurants all over town. People write down their complaints and gripes and anything they want out of their lives. Then the boxes are stuffed inside the Grump and burned so that everyone starts winter with a clean slate. It's a good idea when you think about it."

She nodded. The man and woman were still kissing. Alina couldn't help feeling a little envious. Not that she didn't have a good life, but something was still missing— romance, love, the happily ever after she'd dreamed of since she was a girl, the life she'd been *promised*.

Music blared. The actor in the pink doublet was playing an electric guitar and other musicians had joined him. Alina and Eric were pushed to the edge of the crowd by others who surged forward to dance. Alina looked around for Marissa and spotted her with a lanky intern on whom Marissa had a crush—the real reason the two friends had headed to Vinotok in the first place, since the intern had told them that afternoon he expected to attend.

"Do you ski?" Eric asked when they were far enough from the noise and clamor to talk.

"Ski? Oh, yes." A ski pass was part of her employee benefits in the exchange program between American and Eastern European hospitals. "Yes, I love to ski."

"That's terrific. I'm a ski patroller at Crested Butte Mountain Resort."

"I thought you said you were a paramedic."

"I do both. The jobs go together when you think about it." He had a really nice smile—good teeth and a dimple on the right side of his mouth.

But more than looks drew her to Eric. When his coffee-brown eyes looked into hers, she felt a tug on her heart—a not at all unpleasant sensation. If he could make her feel this way with one look, what else might lay in store for them? She couldn't remember the last time a man had held her attention this way.

"I'm from Gunnison, too," he said. "My family has lived there for years."

"Do you live with your parents?" she asked.

"Yeah. I've thought about getting a place of my own, but it's expensive, and I'd be over there all the time anyway. I guess some people think it's weird, a guy my age still living at home."

"How old are you?" He looked about her age, but it was tough to tell sometimes.

"Twenty-six."

"I'm almost twenty-seven."

There was no mistaking the electricity arcing between them. She couldn't account for this kind of instant connection. It didn't happen outside of books and movies, did it?

"I think it's great that you're close to your family," she said. "If I was in Croatia, I'd still live with my parents. It's expected in our culture that children stay at home until they marry. And as you say, it's practical, too. Housing is expensive."

"Do you have a big family? Brothers and sisters?"

"Two sisters. They're both married now, so only my mother and father and Aunt Oksana are left at home." Which wasn't where she grew up anyway, but a new apartment in downtown Zagreb.

"I have two older sisters," Eric said. "And four older brothers."

"Seven children!" Families so large were rare in Croatia.

"Yeah, it's a big bunch. Of course, they're all married and out of the house now, most of them with kids of their own, so it's just my mom and dad and grandmother and me at home. But we're a pretty close bunch, so at least one of my brothers or sisters and their families are over almost every day."

"That's nice." Alina felt a pang of homesickness. She

missed her own family. On holidays all the women gathered to prepare a big meal and gossip. From the time she could walk she and her sisters were welcomed into this exclusive female territory. They'd be given simple, menial chores like sorting beans or filling salt cellars and would sit for hours, enthralled by the stories, jokes and gossip of the older women. She missed that warm camaraderie, that feeling of being part of a special group, of sharing a family history that went back for centuries.

Those holidays in the family kitchen were when her grandmother Fania had first told her about the blond man she'd one day marry—the one she'd been waiting in vain for all these years.

When Alina was fifteen, her grandmother had announced one morning that she had dreamed Alina's future. No one was surprised at this; *Baka* Fania was known for her ability to predict the future. She had been born with a caul, or a veil of tissue, over her face and had gypsy blood on her grandmother's side—to everyone's way of thinking, it would have been more surprising if she hadn't been able to see things before they happened.

"What kind of future did you see for me?" Alina asked.

"I saw a big blond man, very handsome." The old woman grinned. "He is the key to your future happiness. Find this man and all will be well."

Alina had been looking for the big blond ever since.

"How long have you been in the United States?" Eric asked.

"Almost a year. I came as part of an exchange program for skilled technicians between Croatian hospitals and hospitals in the United States."

Her parents had been horrified when she told them she'd signed up for the program. "No one else in our family has been to the United States," her mother had scolded. "Why do you need to go?"

"I want to see what it's like. To meet new people." Not to mention she'd already dated every eligible man in their small town at least once and none of them had sparked any real feelings in her. Her sisters were happily married with homes of their own, and Alina wanted that, too. Since she hadn't found the man of her dreams in her hometown, she reasoned it was time to be a little more daring and try something new. Some place new.

But she only had three and a half months left before her work visa expired, and her dream man had so far failed to materialize.

Maybe *Baka* Fania had been wrong. Or maybe old-time prophecy didn't apply in the twenty-first century.

"Some friends and family are getting together tomorrow afternoon for a barbecue at my house," Eric said. "You should come."

She started to say no. With only a few months left in the States, she had no business starting anything with a new man, no matter how handsome he was. But Eric's smile made her forget common sense and she found herself nodding. "Yes, I'd like that," she said.

"Great." He patted his pockets. "Do you have a piece of paper? I'll write down the address."

She searched her purse until she found a flyer about upcoming emergency training at the hospital and handed it to him. He scribbled an address and a few lines of directions. "It's really easy to find," he said. "Show up around two. It's going to be fun."

"All right." It would be nice to get to know him better.

"I'm looking forward to seeing you again," Eric said, his eyes locked to hers.

She nodded, struck dumb by the intensity of his gaze and surprised at the strength of her attraction to someone who was so unlike the man of her dreams.

ERIC LINGERED SO LONG at the Vinotok celebration he was almost late for his shift with Gunnison Valley Emergency Medical Services. As he clipped on his radio, his friend Maddie Ansdar emerged from the office. "I was beginning to think you weren't going to show up," she said.

"I stopped by Vinotok," he said.

"How did it go?"

"Silly as usual. Zephyr stole the show with his turn as Sir Hapless."

"What about Max?" Maddie asked. "Wasn't he the Green Man?"

"I thought so, but Jack Crenshaw took his place—and then proposed to Tanya Bledso, right there in front of the burning Grump."

"How romantic!" Maddie's expression took on the soft, goopy look women wore at the mention of weddings, babies or other such subjects. Eric's sisters were no different. And Maddie was probably more susceptible than most, since she'd been married only a few months to Eric's fellow ski patroller, Hagan Ansdar.

"It's crazy if you ask me," Eric said. "What if she'd turned him down?"

"He must have been pretty sure she wouldn't," Maddie said. "Besides, women like men who take risks, didn't you know that?" She grinned.

"And here I thought it was just my ski patrol uniform that attracted them."

"Hey, Eric, Maddie." Marty Padgett, one of their co-workers, strolled in. Over six feet tall with unruly blond curls, Marty had the sweet, round face of a cupid on a wrestler's body.

"Hey, Marty, how's it going?" Eric asked.

"I'm beat." Marty sank into a chair at the table in the center of the employee locker room. "I was up late studying last night. Greek and Hebrew." He made a face. "I'm terrible at languages."

"I have a cousin who's a priest," Eric said. "He's always studying. Very brainy."

Marty looked even more unhappy. "I really just want to preach and help people," he said. "I never thought getting a divinity degree would be so hard."

"If you need to hide back in the ambulance bay and study, we won't tell," Maddie said. "If you're lucky, it'll be a slow night."

Marty shook his head. "A Saturday night? Not likely. I'm off tomorrow. I'll study then."

"You're both coming to my house tomorrow afternoon, right?" Eric asked.

"Sorry. Hagan and I both have to work," Maddie said.

"I'll be there," Marty said. "I'll hit the books after."

"Good. There's somebody I want you to meet."

"Oh?" Maddie looked at him curiously.

Marty laughed. "It's a woman, right? I can tell by your voice."

"Alina Allinova." Her name had a musical quality that delighted him. "A little Croatian respiratory therapist from the hospital. I met her at Vinotok tonight."

"I know the one you're talking about," Marty said. "Very pretty. Sexy voice, too."

"You've talked to her?" Eric felt a pinch of jealousy. Everybody liked Marty—especially women. They were always hanging on him and flirting with him, though he always said he was too busy with school and work to date much.

"Just in passing. She seems nice."

"Croatian, huh?" Maddie said. "How did she end up in Gunnison?"

"Some exchange program with the hospital."

"And you just met her tonight and persuaded her to come to your family's party?" She laughed. "You work fast."

"We really hit it off," he said. He didn't know how to explain what had happened: one minute he'd been laughing at Zephyr's antics and the Vinotok play, the next he'd spotted Alina in the crowd. Everything around him had faded—his sight became fuzzy, sounds muted—as he stared at the most beautiful woman he'd ever seen.

She wasn't supernaturally gorgeous, the way a fashion model or actress might be, but the petite brunette with the heart-shaped face and violet eyes glowed with an inner beauty that drew him like a magnet. Though he rarely had trouble talking to anyone, he'd been a little tongue-tied around her at first. But when she'd smiled at him, his nervousness had evaporated.

"You really are into this girl, aren't you?" Maddie grinned at him. "I've never see you like this."

Eric blinked, and worked to assume an expression of indifference. "She's cute, and I think she misses her family in Croatia, so I thought she'd enjoy hanging out with mine for an afternoon. That's all."

That's all he could afford to think anyway. He liked Alina and looked forward to spending more time with her, but no matter how great she was, he wasn't going to get serious about her.

As if reading his thoughts, Maddie asked, "Does she know you're going to be a doctor?"

"We didn't really talk that long." He didn't start medical school until next fall anyway. What were the odds he'd still be seeing Alina then? He'd never dated any other girl that long, but the thought that he and Alina might not last sent a pang of sadness through him.

"Your parents still giving you a hard time about that?" Marty asked. "Should I not bring it up at the barbecue?"

"Don't bring it up." The good mood Eric had brought to work was evaporating as he thought of his murky future. "It's not that they don't want me to be a doctor— they're worried I can't afford it." Immigrants who had raised their standard of living while avoiding debt, Eric's parents thought he was aiming too high.

He couldn't get serious about a woman right now. He had to concentrate on his studies and medical training. Once all that was out of the way in eight or nine years he could think about settling down.

"Alina and I are just going to hang out, have a little fun," he said. "That's all."

"Love isn't all about timing and planning," Maddie said. "We can't always predict the future."

"I know exactly what my future is going to look like," Eric said. "The same as my parents' and my brothers' and sisters' before me—I'll marry a nice girl from the neighborhood, have a bunch of great kids, though maybe not as many as my parents, and spend my weekends playing ball with the children, barbecuing in the backyard and working on projects around the house."

"Sounds nice," Marty said.

"It will be nice. It's a good life. But first I have to get through med school and internships." When he was Dr. Sepulveda, his family would see he'd made the right decision.

Maddie rolled her eyes.

"What?" Eric asked.

"You guys," she said. "You've got everything all neatly planned out, but life doesn't always work that way. Sometimes the right person comes along when you least expect it."

"Like you and Hagan," Eric said.

"Well…neither one of us was interested in getting married and planning a future together when we first met," she said.

"What changed your mind?" Marty asked.

"I guess love did. We went from not wanting to think about the future, to being unable to imagine one without each other."

"You're reading way too much into this," Eric protested. "I saw a girl I liked and invited her to a barbecue. That's it."

"I'm just saying, you can never be sure about these things," Maddie said. "I've never seen you this excited about a girl you just met."

"You haven't known me that long, either." Yes, he was attracted to Alina, and he wanted to know her better, but no way was he ready to settle down. He and Alina could have some fun together, and right now, that was all he needed.

Chapter Two

"Are you sure it's okay for me to come with you?" Marissa asked as she and Alina headed toward Eric's house Sunday afternoon. "After all, I wasn't invited."

Alina checked the directions Eric had scribbled down for her and flipped on her right blinker. "I can't go to a barbecue at a strange house, with people I don't even know, alone," she said.

"I guess not." Marissa nibbled her lower lip. "Do you think there will be other cute guys there?"

"How should I know?" Alina made the turn, then slowed, reading street signs. Fall had come to the Gunnison Valley in a blaze of yellow, orange and red. Aspens and cottonwoods painted the landscape in fiery color, and already scarecrows and pumpkins and other decorations were beginning to show up on front porches.

Eric's neighborhood was one of older, comfortable homes, mixed with newer residences. Children played in front yards and raced bicycles down the street. Alina smiled at a dark-haired little boy who waved at her from the end of his driveway.

"Maybe Eric has brothers who are even better-looking than he is," Marissa said. "Though that's hard to imagine. The man is *hot*." She made a show of fanning herself.

"He's okay," Alina said. Her grandmother would have warned she'd be struck down by lightning for telling such a lie.

"Okay?" Marissa laughed. "Croatia must be full of amazing men if Eric only rates okay."

"Maybe Eric is a little more than okay." A thrill raced through her at the words. Eric was most definitely special if her initial attraction to him was any measure. If he were blond getting together with him would make a better story, considering *Baka* Fania's prophecy, but then, life seldom worked out so neatly.

Alina told herself she was too modern to believe in old superstitions, but doubt pinched at her whenever she thought of her dear grandmother. *Baka* Fania had never been wrong about any of her predictions. She had foreseen each of Alina's sisters' husbands: the big Russian her eldest sister, Radinka, had wed, and the red-headed Scottish businessman her other sister, Zora, had married. Zora had laughed when *Baka* Fania had announced she would spend the rest of her life with a redhead. Very few Croatians had red hair. "Besides, I hate redheads," she'd protested.

But the very next year, Baen McKay had come to town, and Zora had known immediately that he was the one. "You can't fight what was meant to be," she told everyone, and they all agreed that happiness could be found if you paid attention to *Baka's* predictions.

If *Baka* Fania said Alina's husband would be blond, where did that leave handsome, charming, dark-haired Eric Sepulveda?

It left him safe, she decided. She wasn't going to marry Eric, only have a little fun.

"I think you missed the turn."

"What?" Alina snatched the directions from Marissa's hand and studied them. "It says to turn on Clarkson," she said.

"Clarkson is about a block behind us." Marissa pointed behind them.

Grumbling to herself, Alina turned the car around and headed back. She knew the right house the moment she turned onto the street, which was crowded with cars, trucks and vans on either side of the low brick ranch on the left side of the cul-de-sac. She pulled her compact car into a space half a block away and shut off the engine.

"Maybe we should have brought something with us," she said as she studied the people who streamed into the house. Many of them carried coolers or covered bowls or platters.

"It'll be okay," Marissa said. "There are lots of people here. I bet they'll have plenty." She opened the door, but when Alina didn't move, she paused. "What's wrong? Aren't you going to come in?"

"I'm a little nervous, that's all." Ever since they'd set out this morning, a curious energy had raced through her body, leaving every sense hyperalert. She couldn't shake the feeling that today was really important—the kind of day that could change her life forever. Marissa might not understand, but Alina came from a family that respected intuition. When you had a grandmother who was known as a seer, people in her culture took it for granted you had a few gifts of your own.

"Come on," Marissa said. "You can't just sit out here. The sooner you get past the introductions, the sooner we'll start having fun."

"You're right." Nervous yet wanting to know what lay ahead, she followed Marissa across a yard strewn with children and toys. They followed a group of people through the open front door. She had a brief impression of comfortable furniture and rooms full of people before they emerged into the sunlit backyard. Mexican music blared from a radio balanced on a card table on the deck, while a group of men gathered around an enormous barbecue pit in a back corner. Voices spoke in Spanish and English, and the air was redolent with the aroma of smoking meat and spices.

"Alina!"

Eric strode toward her. Dressed in faded jeans and a black polo shirt, he was easily one of the handsomest men in attendance. He caught and held her gaze as he moved toward her, and briefly she forgot about everything except him and her wildly pounding heart.

"I'm glad you could make it," he said. He surprised her by pulling her close for a quick, strong hug.

"Thank you." She carefully—and somewhat reluctantly—extricated herself from his embrace. "It's good to see you, too."

The sharp pain of Marissa's elbow in her side reminded Alina they weren't alone. "This is my friend,

Marissa Alvarez," Alina said. "She's a nurse at the hospital. I hope you don't mind I brought her along."

"No, that's great. This is my friend Marty Padgett."

For the first time Alina noticed the man standing next to Eric. She stared at him, and might have stopped breathing for a second. Marty was tall and broad and very blond, with a face like an angel.

"Hi, Alina." Marty offered a meaty hand. "I bet you don't remember me, but I've seen you at the hospital."

She took the hand he offered, and waited for the tingle she was sure would surge through her—the signal that this was the man her grandmother had predicted would make her happy. Just because she didn't really believe in the prophecy didn't mean she'd pass up a chance at true love, happiness and the whole romance package.

But she experienced no particular sensation, except that Marty had kind of a weak handshake for such a big guy.

"Let me show you where everything is and introduce you to some people." Eric took her arm and led her across the yard. Marissa and Marty trailed after them.

Alina glanced over her shoulder and saw that Marissa had her arm linked with Marty's and was flirting with him in that open, friendly way of hers. Men always liked Marissa, with her fall of long dark hair and friendly smile.

The little procession halted in front of a half-dozen men and women who'd gathered in the shade of a spreading oak. "Everyone, this is Alina Allinova and her friend, Marissa Alvarez." Eric turned to Marissa. "This is my brother John and my brother Bart and their wives,

Renee and Sabina, and my sister Sofia and her husband, Guillermo."

"Like you're going to remember all that, right?" A stocky thirtysomething extended a hand. "Just remember that I'm the older, handsome brother," he said. "Bart here—" he jerked his thumb at a slightly younger man with curly dark hair "—he's the clown. Eric is the baby."

"Some baby." A slender woman with artfully streaked blond hair rolled her eyes and offered her hand also. "I'm Sofia, married to this big lug." She nudged the shoulder of a short, barrel-chested man who grinned at her fondly. "We have three little boys running around here somewhere, but don't bother trying to keep them straight. They're all little wild men."

"Sofia is closest to Eric in age," John said. "She's the youngest sister, but the bossiest."

"Men need *someone* to tell them what to do." Sofia gestured to her brothers. "They pretend to protest, but they'd be lost without us."

Alina smiled and shook hands and tried to keep track of the many people and names. "How did an ugly sucker like my brother end up with two beautiful women as his guests?" Bart asked. "Tell the truth, ladies—did he bribe you to show up?"

"Can I help it if I got all the charm in the family?" Eric winked at Alina and she felt a warm tickle of attraction.

"It's very nice to meet you all," she said.

"We'll have a little girl talk later," Sofia said. "I want to hear all the dirt on my little brother."

"Ignore her. There is no dirt." Eric took Alina's arm. "Come on. I want you to meet Mom and Pop."

At the mention of his parents, Alina's stomach gave a nervous shimmy. What if they didn't like her? What if they were upset their son had invited a stranger to their home like this?

"Who is this?" demanded a short, broad man with Eric's dimpled smile as the trio approached. He wore a black apron that proclaimed him King of the Grill.

"Dad, this is Alina Allinova and Marissa Alvarez," Eric said.

"Bienvenidos," Mr. Sepulveda boomed. "Welcome." He shook both their hands. "Eric should bring such pretty women home more often."

Alina flushed, touched by such an effusive welcome. "Thank you for hosting us," she said, hoping she had the words right. She still struggled with English sometimes.

"Yes, this is a terrific party," Marissa said. She made a sweeping motion with her hand, taking in the tables laden with food, groups of laughing children and crowd of adults gathered in the shady yard.

"We like to entertain," Mr. Sepulveda said with a modest shrug of his shoulders. "Join us anytime."

"And this is my grandmother Torres." Eric led them to a bent, plump woman with a crown of silver braids. *"Abuelita,* this is Alina Allinova and Marissa Alvarez."

Mrs. Torres nodded regally, and said something to her grandson in Spanish.

"She doesn't speak English." Marty leaned closer to Alina and whispered. "Though I suspect she understands it well enough."

With a stab of pain, Alina thought of *Baka* Fania, who had died two years before. She, too, had never learned

English, saying that since she was good at reading people's hearts, she had no need to understand their tongues, as well.

Mrs. Torres stared at Alina as if trying to read her heart. Alina managed a weak smile. Mrs. Torres said something and Alina looked to Eric for a translation. "She said she's pleased to meet you," Eric said. Though something in his manner made Alina suspect those had not been the old woman's exact words.

Eric kissed his grandmother's cheek, then led them and Marty to a shaded arbor crowded with benches and lawn chairs. "And this is my mother," he said, introducing an older blonde who wore a long flowered skirt and white blouse. Though lines around her eyes and mouth testified to her age, Mrs. Sepulveda had clearly been a beauty in her younger years. "Mama, this is Alina Allinova and Marissa Alvarez."

Mrs. Sepulveda smiled warmly. "It's so nice to meet you both," she said. "How do you girls know Eric and Marty?"

Alina was slow to answer, overwhelmed at meeting so many new people at once. Marissa jumped in to fill the silence. "Alina's a respiratory therapist and I'm an RN at the hospital," she said.

Mrs. Sepulveda studied Marissa thoughtfully. "Are you related to Frank and Millie Alvarez?" she asked.

"I don't think so. My family is from Pueblo."

"I have a lot of friends in Pueblo. Why don't you girls sit here beside me and we'll find out if we know any of the same people. Eric, fetch us something to drink."

While Marissa and Mrs. Sepulvida conversed in a

mixture of Spanish and English, Alina took a seat on a nearby bench. Marty joined her. Here was her chance to get to know him better. "How do you know Eric?" she asked.

"We work together—I'm a paramedic, too."

"Then I'm amazed I haven't run into you at the hospital. I'm sure I'd remember." Because of her grandmother's prophecy, every blond man she saw made an impression on her, but she had no memory of this one, though he'd claimed to have met her before.

"You'd be amazed how many people don't remember me. I guess because I'm kind of quiet."

"I'm a quiet person, too," she said. When she'd first come to the United States, she'd avoided speaking because she'd been worried about betraying her ignorance of English, though she'd studied the language for years. But even at home she had always preferred listening to and watching others, never needing to be the center of attention. "And I like quiet men," she added. "Better than ones who talk too much."

"Eric doesn't talk too much," Marty said. "He's a great guy."

Eric again. The man who really made her heart race. But she felt she owed it to her grandmother to at least give Marty a chance. "Eric is very nice," she murmured. "But—"

"He's a lot of fun and really down-to-earth, too," Marty continued. "In spite of being such a daredevil."

"I don't understand." Alina wasn't sure what the term meant.

"It just means someone who likes to take risks. Eric likes skiing out of bounds or in extreme terrain, and in the summer he races motorcycles and climbs mountains—that kind of thing."

She hated the idea of Eric risking his life on a motorcycle. She'd recently cared for a young man who'd been seriously injured in a motorcycle accident. She pushed the thought away. She shouldn't focus on Eric, the handsome risk-taker. She needed to get to know Marty, to determine if he was the man who would make her happy for the rest of her life. "What do you like to do when you're not working?" she asked.

"I'm going to school, studying to be a minister."

"A…a minister?" Not what she'd expected. The opposite of being a daredevil, she supposed.

"You know, a preacher. A reverend."

"That's nice." Even to her ears, the words sounded weak.

"Not exactly the world's sexiest profession." He laughed. "But an important one, I think."

"Yes. Of course."

She waited for him to pick up the conversation, but he merely smiled at her blandly. That was definitely one drawback to two quiet people trying to get to know each other.

Eric returned, drinks in hand, and a little girl in tow. One of his nieces, she thought. "This is Emma," he introduced the tyke as he handed the drinks around. "Say hello to Alina and Marissa."

"He-wo," the child said, the word muffled by the thumb stuck in her mouth.

"How old are you, Emma?" Alina asked.

The little girl looked questioningly at her uncle.

"She's three," Mrs. Sepulveda said. "And Eric is her favorite uncle."

"She has good taste," Marissa said. She winked at Alina, who quickly looked away.

"Uncle Eric, I want up." Emma stretched her arms skyward and stood on tiptoe.

"Emma, you're too big for me to hold all the time," he said, even as he bent to gather her in his arms.

"I like it up here 'cause I'm tall." She grinned at the circle of adults.

Alina couldn't help but grin back, not only at the adorable little girl, but at the picture of the child nestled against Eric, who held her with such tenderness. Before her eyes the ladies' man who had flirted with her at Vinotok—the man who risked his life racing motorcycles and skiing off cliffs and no telling what else—had transformed into an easygoing family man, beloved by grandparents and toddlers alike. What woman wouldn't be charmed?

"There you are!" One of the women Alina had met earlier—Renee—hurried to them. "Stop bothering Uncle Eric and let him visit with his friends."

"I wasn't bothering him!" Emma protested.

"She really wasn't," Eric said, though he handed her over to her mother.

"Let's go fix you a plate," Renee said. "Papa made some little sausages especially for you."

Effectively distracted, Emma went willingly with her mother. Eric squeezed in beside Alina on the bench so that she had to move over toward Marty to accommodate him. She was aware of how close she was, not to Marty, but to Eric, their thighs touching. He glanced toward his mother and Marissa, who were deep in conversation once more. "I don't think Mom meant to leave you out in the cold," he said.

"Oh, it's all right," Alina said. "Marissa's like that. She can talk to anyone about anything."

Whereas the three of them suddenly had nothing to say. Alina, aware of both men watching her, was struck by the truth of the saying "three's a crowd." Marty might be the type of man her grandmother had decreed she should be attracted to, but Eric drew her the way she imagined the forbidden fruit had once tempted Eve.

ERIC'S DAD ANNOUNCED that the meat was ready, and Eric was pressed into service helping to fill plates with smoky chicken, spicy chorizo sausage and slices of beef brisket. As he worked, he darted glances at Alina and Marissa, who had found a spot at one of the big tables with some of Eric's sisters and his brothers' wives.

"She's very pretty." His brother John accepted a plate of brisket from Eric and nodded to Alina. "What's the story with you two?"

"I met her at Vinotok last night and invited her to come to the barbecue," Eric said. "There is no story."

"She's good-looking." Bart joined them. "I noticed the accent. Where's she from?"

"Croatia." He sliced chorizo into bite-size pieces and transferred them to a young nephew's plate.

"She's a long way from home," Bart said.

"She's here on an exchange program with the hospital."

"So she'll be going home eventually." John nodded as if this was significant.

"In a few months," Eric said.

Bart grinned. "That explains it, then."

"Explains what?"

"Why you're staring at her and not her pretty Latina friend." John popped a bite of chicken into his mouth.

"What's that supposed to mean?"

"We know you, bro," Bart said. "You don't date women who are wife material. It's how you've managed to remain single longer than any of the rest of us."

"And it's why Mama is getting worried," John said. "Didn't you see the way her eyes lit up when you introduced her to Marissa? She doesn't know yet Alina is the one you're really interested in."

"If you're nice to us, we won't tell her the truth." Bart's grin was wicked. "Yet."

"You're imagining things." Eric attacked the brisket with renewed vigor.

"No, we're not." John's expression grew serious. "Mama is desperate to see her baby married and settled down."

"Why does she automatically assume Marissa is the one I should marry?" Eric asks.

"Not Marissa specifically," Bart said. "But she fits the profile."

"What profile?"

"Don't play dumb," Bart said. "You know the drill. You find a nice girl from the same background and culture, get married and build a life just like the one your parents built."

"It's the way we do things," John said.

Eric thought of his brothers and sisters, who had all followed this pattern. Though he would never admit it to his brothers, he'd assumed he would take much the same path. While he enjoyed taking risks in his leisure activities and even on the job, he saw no reason to be reckless when it came to his personal life. His brothers and sisters were all happy; his parents were happy. Why shouldn't this same approach make Eric happy, too?

He respected his family's history and admired all his parents had done. They were leaders in the community. His dad's machine shop was a gathering place for local men, and his mother was active in the church and the local community center. Eric would be proud to pattern his life after theirs—but not just yet.

"There's nothing wrong with having fun with pretty women," John said. "But you ought to think about settling down soon."

"If you don't, Mama and Grandmother will find a wife for you," Bart said. "You don't want that."

"Remember what happened to Gilberto," John said.

"What happened to Gilberto?" Eric looked across the yard to where his eldest brother stood with a group of older men. Gilberto had been married for years— apparently happily—to a large, cheerful woman who had come into the machine shop one day to pick up parts for her father.

"You're too young to remember," John said. "When he was twenty, he made the mistake of telling Mama that he didn't plan on getting married until he was thirty because he was having too much fun being single and didn't want the burden of a family."

Eric tried to imagine anyone in his family making this kind of announcement to his parents; he couldn't. He and his brothers and sisters might think such things, but why say them out loud and risk an argument? "What happened?" he asked.

"Mama said that was fine. That no one should be *burdened* by a family," Bart said.

"Then she and *Abuelita* were like generals on the attack." John took up the story again. "Soon Gilberto couldn't turn around without being confronted by some eligible young woman. They attended every family dinner. They sat next to him at church. Mama persuaded Papa to hire a new secretary at the shop, the daughter of a friend. If Gilberto tried to get away, to play soccer with his friends or to have a drink at a tavern, Mama would show up with some young woman in tow."

"He was miserable," Bart said. "He finally had to admit he'd have no peace until he got engaged."

"So Maria was one of the young women sent to him by Mama and Grandmother?" Eric asked.

"No. I guess they hadn't heard of her yet." Bart laughed. "She was new in town and when Gilberto realized this, he decided she had to be the one. Then at least he could say he'd chosen her of his own free will."

"After that, the rest of us knew we didn't stand a chance," John said. "We made our own choices and it's worked out for the best."

"It's only because you're the baby and her favorite that Mama and Grandmother have held off so long,"

Bart said. "But if you don't show some signs of settling down soon, they're going to make their move."

"When the time comes, I'll make my own choice, too," Eric said. "But I have to finish medical school first. It's going to take everything I have to get through that. I won't have the time or energy for a relationship."

"So you're still set on being a doctor," John said.

"Why would you think I'd changed my mind? It's what I've wanted for years."

"I wanted to be an astronaut once, too," Bart said. "But you don't see me walking on the moon."

"Mama's even more upset about the idea of you going away to medical school than she is about you still being single," John said. "She wants you here at home, out of debt and settled down, raising more grandchildren."

John nodded. "I wouldn't be surprised if she and *Abuelita's* New Year's resolutions don't involve finding you a wife."

Eric opened his mouth to deny this. The whole idea was preposterous, especially in this day and age. No one could force a woman on him.

Except his grandmother's words when he'd introduced Alina to her still echoed in his head. Words he hadn't dared translate for Alina: "She's a very pretty girl, but when are you going to bring home someone you can be serious about?"

IF YOU WANTED to really get to know a man, Alina decided, there were worse ways than spending time with his sisters. While Alina and Marissa stuffed themselves with brisket and beans, chorizo and *chilliquillas,* Eric's sisters Sofia and Cari, along with his sisters-in-law Renee and Sabina, regaled them with stories of Eric's exploits—from the time he ate a batch of cookies their mother had made and tried to blame it on the family cat, to harrowing accidents on his motorcycle, to the time he'd dressed in drag for a school play.

Alina was still laughing at the mental image of Eric in a wig and falsies when he joined them, Marty trailing behind.

"What have you two been up to?" Marissa asked, scooting over to make room for them. "We were beginning to feel abandoned."

"I knew it was a mistake to leave you alone too long." Eric squeezed in between them. "My sisters have probably been telling all kinds of lies about me."

"Only the truth," Sofia said, grinning. "They both know they'd be wise to stay far away from you."

"That isn't fair," Eric said. "There's no one here to tell stories on Marty."

"There's nothing to tell," Marty said. "Compared to Eric, I've led a very unexciting life."

"Alina has had more adventures than any of us," Marissa said. "I've never even been out of Colorado, and she came all the way from Croatia to live here."

"What made you decide to come to the United States?" Cari asked.

"It was a great opportunity to see new places, meet new people and learn some new skills." As much as she loved her country and her family and all their traditions, she'd begun to feel smothered by them. She'd wanted the chance to live truly independently—to make decisions based not on what had always been done but on what she wanted.

"And you're here for a whole year?" Sofia asked.

"Until mid-January, yes."

Marissa shook her head. "I'd miss my family and friends too much to leave for that long," she said. "I mean, my three sisters drove me crazy when we were growing up, but the toughest thing about going off to college was getting used to not having them around anymore."

"I was very homesick at first," Alina admitted. "And I do miss my family. But I think being away from them has made me appreciate them more."

"Maybe I should get away from my family for a while," Eric said. "So I could try that appreciation thing."

Sofia stuck her tongue out at him. "You'd be lost without us, little brother."

Alina turned to Marty. "What about your family?" she asked. "Where do they live?"

"They're in Denver," he said. "I have an older sister, who's married and lives in Connecticut." He shrugged. "Not much else to tell."

But surely there was, Alina thought. What were their names? What did they do for a living? Did he miss them? Did he want to move back to Denver to be near his parents when he'd finished his studies? But she didn't want to fire all these questions at him at once, afraid to appear she was interrogating him.

"I'm glad you decided to come to the United States," Eric said. "If you hadn't, we wouldn't have gotten the chance to get to know you." The words were innocent enough, but the unspoken message behind them was that *he* wanted to know her much better.

Unnerved by how much that idea pleased her, she excused herself and carried her empty plate and utensils to the trash barrels set up by the back gate. Marissa followed her. "Don't leave me," Marissa whispered. "I have to hide from Eric's mom."

"His mom? Why?"

Marissa glanced around, then, apparently deciding they were out of earshot of anyone else, said, "She wants to fix me up with her son."

"With one of Eric's brothers?" Hadn't he told her all his siblings were married?

"No, with Eric!"

"Eric?" She had a hard time getting the word out, so stunned was she by this idea.

"Yes. Can you believe it?"

Alina swallowed, and forced a lightness she didn't feel into her voice. "I thought you liked him. You said he was cute."

"Yes, but I'd never poach on a friend's guy." Marissa shook her head. "That's just wrong."

The news flooded Alina with relief, though she fought against it. "I do like Eric," she said. "But we only just met. He's not exactly my guy."

Marissa gave her a pitying look. "He's really into you. Don't pretend you haven't noticed."

Yes, she'd noticed. She'd have to be in a coma not to. And she was definitely interested in him. He was kind and funny and good-looking and sexy...but was he the right man for her? She was a modern, independent woman—but deep down she wanted to believe her grandmother's prophecy, that there was one particular man pre-ordained to make her happy. "What do you think of Marty?" she asked.

Marissa shrugged. "He's okay. But he's kind of…dull."

Marty didn't have Eric's charisma, that was true. "He seems very sweet," Alina said.

"Yeah, but I like a little more spice with my sweet, if you know what I mean."

Eric was plenty spicy. Alina turned to watch him as he pretended to wrestle with one of his young nephews. The longer she was around him, the more she felt her resistance to him weakening. The two of them could have a lot of fun together. But she was leaving in three months. What would happen then?

Chapter Three

The problem with inviting Alina to the barbecue, Eric decided, was that he hadn't found any opportunity to be alone with her. After his conversation with his brothers, he'd been acutely aware of everyone watching whenever he so much as looked at Alina.

"So I have to find a way to ask her out without it really being a date," he explained to Marty as the two cruised around town in an ambulance the following Monday. They'd taken the vehicle in for an oil change and were now driving the long way back to the station.

"Why not just ask her out on a date?" Marty asked.

"Because if I do that, word will get back to my mother and grandmother, and they'll decide to take matters into their own hands."

"What are you talking about?" Marty asked.

"My mother and grandmother have decided it's time I was married," he said.

"Why now?" Marty asked.

"I'm the only one of my siblings who isn't married. Also, I suspect my mom thinks if I'm married I'll settle down and give up the idea of going away to medical school."

"I thought every mother wanted her son to be a doctor."

"Believe me, when I'm a doctor she'll be proud as can be. But she thinks I'm too ambitious, that I'm going to get in over my head, incur a mountain of debt, kill myself studying and working, become estranged from my family… If there's a worst-case scenario, my mother has imagined it."

"So she wants you to marry and settle down here in Gunnison. I get that. Then they ought to be happy if you start dating someone, shouldn't they?"

"Only if it's the right someone."

"And Alina isn't the right someone?"

"Alina is from another country—and plans to return there in a few months." The knowledge made his stomach hurt.

"Ah. And your folks want you to settle down with a cute little Latina."

"Exactly. So you see my problem."

Marty shook his head. "Not really. Going out with a woman doesn't mean you're going to marry her. And you're twenty-six years old. What's your mother going to do—send you to bed without your supper?"

"Very funny. You don't know my mother. And my grandmother is twice as bad. When I was ten and decided I didn't like green beans, she served them to me every night for six months. It was easier to give in and choke them down than face six more months of seeing them on my plate every time I sat down to dinner."

"There's a big difference between a vegetable and

the woman you'll spend the rest of your life with," Marty said.

"My mother and grandmother can be relentless when they're trying to make a point," Eric said. "If I start dating Alina, they'll set me up with other women they think are more suitable. Every time I turn around one will just 'happen' to be there. Alina will think I'm some kind of playboy."

"I guess Alina wouldn't like that," Marty said.

"Especially not when we hardly know each other," Eric said. "The only chance I have is if the two of us can become friends before my family has a chance to interfere."

"Then whatever your family does, she'll be so besotted it won't matter?" Marty said.

Or maybe *he'd* be so enamored he'd find a way to stand up to his folks. "I just want us to be able to have a good time before she has to go back to Croatia, that's all," he said. Though he hated to admit it, there was some truth in what his brothers had said—part of his interest in Alina probably lay in the fact that any relationship with her was destined to be temporary.

But since she was leaving soon, he couldn't afford to waste any time he might spend with her now.

A loud tone from the radio alerted them to a call. "Elderly woman needs assistance at Lifeway Manor, two-one-one-two West Virginia Avenue."

Eric and Marty exchanged a look. "The bowling ladies," Marty said.

"Yeah, the bowling ladies," Eric said grimly, and switched on the siren and flashing lights.

"Copy, dispatch. We're on our way," Marty said.

Lifeway Manor was an assisted-living facility not far from downtown. The elderly residents were mostly independent, living in separate apartments with access to a central dining facility, an on-site medical clinic and a host of planned activities.

The newest addition to the activity schedule, and the cause of great excitement among the residents, was a series of baseball games, golf tournaments and other games which the residents could "play" thanks to the latest video game technology. With these games, even wheelchair-bound residents could take to the links or to the basketball court. This had led to the formation of teams and a healthy competition among the residents.

But no group was more rabid or competitive than the women's bowling league. The nineteen women who competed in the bowling tournaments battled with such intensity that several of them were familiar faces to members of the Gunnison Valley Emergency Medical Services crews.

First had been Carla Polenski, who had thrown out her shoulder while bowling a virtual strike. Then Betty Peabody had gotten stuck in the elevator when she pressed all the buttons at once in her haste not to be late to a scheduled game. Pearl Winters had fainted when her blood pressure spiked during an argument over scoring.

Tonight's casualty was one June Freed, a pleasant-faced munchkin of a woman who had fallen in her rush to reach the game room ahead of her archrival Opal Simpson. "She always gets there first and camps out in my favorite chair," June griped as Eric examined her swollen arm. "I'm sick and tired of it, I tell you."

"It looks like your arm might be broken," Eric said. "You'll need to have an X ray to know for sure. Do you want us to take you to the hospital in the ambulance?"

"No. I already called my son. He'll take me. But not before the tournament is over."

"Why don't you just take the game away from them?" Eric asked the harried administrator as he completed the required paperwork at the nurse's station.

"Oh, I couldn't do that." The administrator's eyes widened. "They'd revolt. When the golf game malfunctioned for two weeks, some of the men staged a sit-in in the main dining room. They threatened to call the newspapers if we didn't have the game repaired immediately. One of them even said he'd have his grandson film a protest for YouTube."

"Maybe you should take Alina bowling," Marty said as he and Eric headed back toward the station. "It's obviously a more exciting game than I imagined."

Eric gave him a sour look.

"So what are you going to do about her?" Marty persisted.

"We need to do something with friends that still provides the opportunity for the two of us to be alone." Eric glanced at his friend. "What do you think of Marissa?"

Marty blinked. "I don't know. She seems nice enough. Why?"

"You should ask her to come with us. That will help Alina feel more at ease." He flipped on his blinker for the turn into the station.

"*Us?* Since when am I involved in this?"

"Since now." Eric backed the ambulance into its bay, ready for the next call-out.

Maddie came out to meet them. "I just heard from Hagan," she said. "It's snowing in the high country. They could get eight to ten inches tonight."

"That's perfect," Eric said.

"Spoken like a man who doesn't have to shovel his driveway," Marty said.

"No, this is great. Maddie, you and Hagan have a snowmobile, don't you?"

"Sure. You want to borrow it?"

"No, my brothers have a couple we can use. Would you and Hagan like to go snowmobiling this weekend? We could ask Max and Casey and some other folks— make a party of it."

"Okay." Maddie looked from one man to the other. "Why do I get the feeling there's more behind this than the desire to take advantage of the fresh snow?"

"Eric doesn't care about the rest of us," Marty said. "We're just giving him an excuse to romance Alina Allinova."

"Since when do you need all of us to do that?" Maddie asked.

"It's a long story."

"I've got time." She crossed her arms and leaned back against the ambulance.

"Just let me know if you're free to go snowmobiling with us this weekend."

"I wouldn't miss it," she said. "I'm anxious to meet a woman who has you calling in reinforcements."

ALINA HAD ENROLLED in technical college with the intention of training to be an X ray technician. A friend had explained this was the perfect career, offering high pay and flexible hours.

But the introductory course she needed had been full, and the student counselor had convinced her to try a respiratory therapist course instead. After one evening clinic at the hospital, watching her instructor assist a little girl with asthma and an elderly man with emphysema, Alina was hooked. Taking pictures and developing film seemed boring in comparison to saving lives by helping people to breathe.

Already on this Tuesday evening she'd treated an accident victim with a collapsed lung, done a blood gas analysis on another patient and administered breathing treatments to three patients, including Mr. Herrerra, an elderly man with chronic obstructive pulmonary disorder. "Your oxygen levels are much better today," she said, removing the pulse oxymeter from Mr. Herrera's finger. "If you keep improving this way, you'll be going home in no time."

"I wish the home health aide that comes to my house was as pretty as you are," he said.

"I bet you say that to all the women." She stowed the pulse oxymeter and packed up the nebulizer. "You have a good night, and a safe trip home if I don't see you tomorrow."

She wheeled the cart with her supplies back into the corridor to the nurses' station, where she could record her activities and findings in Mr. Herrerra's chart. A small window nearby looked out onto the hospital parking lot and a lacy curtain of snowflakes illuminated by the floodlights.

She thought she'd known winter before coming to Colorado. After all, Croatia had mountains and plenty of snow. But she'd never seen a winter like her first in Gunnison. Snow piled higher than the roofs and the turning lanes of the streets filled with great drifts pushed there by the plows. Temperatures hovered near zero for weeks at a time, while the sun glared off everything, bright but giving little warmth.

Despite the chill, people embraced the weather, devoting themselves to every kind of activity involving snow, from skiing and sledding to ice sculpture competitions and snowshoe races.

"Mr. Herrerra says he's in love." Marissa stood at Alina's elbow. Dressed in raspberry-pink scrubs, a stethoscope draped around her neck, she was the picture of the efficient nurse.

"With you?" Alina asked.

"A little bit with me. Mostly with you. You have another conquest."

"A seventy-seven-year-old boyfriend. I'm so flattered."

"Speaking of boyfriends, have you seen Eric lately?"

"No." She'd thought of him often since Sunday; the sight of dark hair and the red shirts of the Gunnison Valley EMS was enough to make her heart race and her head turn.

"You could always call him," Marissa said.

"No, I could not."

"Of course you could."

"But I don't want to." If he was really as interested as Marissa had said, he would have called *her*.

"But you could."

"Enough, Marissa. I have work to do."

"Did you hear Amy Fremont is leaving after the first of the year?"

"Really?" Amy was head of the respiratory therapy department at Gunnison Valley Hospital.

"Her husband's retiring and they're building a house near Lake Powell."

"How do you know these things?" Alina asked.

Marissa shrugged. "I hear stuff. For instance, I know Eric Sepulveda has never been involved with anyone."

Eric again. "Never? Not even a high school crush?"

"I mean, *seriously* involved. No engagements. Never lived with anyone. He's dated a lot, but never any one woman for very long."

"That's not so unusual." She'd never been engaged or *involved* with anyone, either. Not for lack of trying— she'd dated a number of men, but had never fallen in love with any of them.

"He's the youngest in his family and the only one who isn't married."

"I'm the only one in my family who isn't married," Alina said. "And you're not married, either."

"I'm the oldest in my family. You're the youngest. And so is Eric. See—you have lots in common." Marissa sounded positively gleeful.

"Why are you so interested in me and Eric?" Alina asked. "I've been here eight months and you haven't cared who I dated or didn't date."

"I have a good feeling about you two," Marissa said. "And didn't you know I'm a hopeless romantic?"

"Hopeless is right."

"Hi. Are you Alina Allinova?"

Alina started, and saw a woman with brown curly hair moving down the corridor toward her. The newcomer wore the red shirt and dark pants of the Emergency Medical Service. "Y-yes. I'm Alina," she stammered.

"I'm Maddie Ansdar." The woman offered her hand. "I just transported a patient here, and I've heard so much about you I wanted to meet you."

"Heard about her from *whom?*" Marissa asked.

"Oh, different people." Maddie sketched a vague gesture in the air. "I understand you're from Croatia. I skied there several times—at Bjelolasica."

Alina's eyes widened. Most people she'd met had never heard of Bjelolasica, much less knew how to pronounce it. "My family went there on vacations several times when I was younger," she said. In college, groups of friends had often rented chalets for the weekend, skiing all day and partying into the night. Those days felt very long ago.

"I didn't get to see much of the country other than the slopes," Maddie said. "But what I saw was beautiful."

"We never saw many Americans there," Alina said. "Most of them prefer to travel to the Alps in France or Italy."

"I was on the U.S. Olympic team and competed in some World Cup races there," Maddie said. "At least I did until I injured my leg."

"And now you're in Gunnison. Are you from here?"

Maddie shook her head. "I live in Crested Butte. I

worked for the ski patrol for a while and met my husband and decided to stay."

"You must know Eric and Marty," Marissa said.

"I do." Maddie looked at Alina expectantly.

Alina felt as if she were in a play where everyone knew their lines but her. "Well, it was nice to meet you, Maddie," she said.

"Have you talked to Eric lately?" Maddie asked.

"No. Should I have?"

"Oh, I imagine you will soon."

The idea pleased Alina. "When you see him, tell him I said hello."

"I'll do that." The women said goodbye and Alina turned back to her paperwork.

"This is looking good," Marissa said. "He's been talking about you to his coworkers. He's crazy about you."

"He can't get too crazy," Alina said. "I'm only going to be here until January."

"A lot can happen in a few months. You might decide this is true love."

"Oh, please!" Alina protested, even as her heart pounded. "You told me Eric has never had a serious girlfriend and he's the only one of his siblings who hasn't been married. Does that sound like the kind of man who wants to settle down to you?"

"Yes. He's sown all his wild oats and is ready to fall in love. And I think you're the woman he's fallen in love with."

Alina's heart stomped out a frenzied folk dance. "The man hardly knows me."

Marissa shrugged. "Some people are meant to be together."

So her grandmother had always said. And according to *Baka* Fania, the person Alina was meant to be with was a big, good-looking blond. Someone like Marty—who as far as Alina could tell was a sweet, shy, absolutely *boring* man who generated not a single spark in her. And none of the other blond men she'd dated over the years had sparked any feelings in her, either.

So much for grandmother knowing best.

ERIC KNEW he made a good impression in his dark jeans and leather jacket. Female heads turned as he passed through the corridors of Gunnison Valley Hospital Wednesday afternoon, and he resisted the urge to stop and flirt with the prettier nurses, aides and one attractive female surgeon. He had a mission to accomplish and he couldn't afford to be distracted.

He found Alina in the hallway outside a patient's room, marking something on the chart by the door. "Hey," he said, and stopped beside her.

Her pale complexion blushed prettily, reminding him of a fast-motion film of a rose blooming. "Hello," she said. "What are you doing here?"

"I came to see you. How are you doing?"

"I'm fine." She clicked her pen several times rapidly before shoving it into the pocket of her pale blue scrubs. "What can I do for you?"

"A group of us are going snowmobiling this weekend up by Kebler Pass. I'm hoping you can go with us."

"Oh, I don't know. I…I'll have to check my schedule."

"I talked to Marissa, and she thought you might be free Saturday," Eric said. "She's coming with us. So is Marty and some other people, mostly from Crested Butte. But they're great folks. You'll like them."

Alina hesitated.

"Have you been snowmobiling before?" he asked. "It's a lot of fun."

"No, I haven't."

"Then you should come. Who knows when you'll have the chance again?"

"All right," she said. "I'd like that."

"Great. I'll pick you up about eight Saturday morning."

"All right. I'll give you my address."

"No problem. I already got it from Marissa."

She looked surprised, but said nothing. Eric would like to be a fly on the wall when she talked to Marissa about that. "I guess I'll see you then," she said.

Clearly she expected him to leave, but he lingered, reluctant to break off their conversation. This was the longest they'd ever spent alone, and he wanted to make the most of it. He followed her to the supply closet and watched while she replenished the supplies on her cart. "What made you decide to become a respiratory therapist?" he asked.

"I liked that it was a way to really help people," she said. "Patients come to me, unable to breathe, and I can make a real difference for them."

"Why not a doctor or a nurse?"

She shrugged. "That took money and training I didn't have. This was more immediate. More specialized. A doctor has to know everything. I'm able to concentrate on doing this one thing well. And it's very hands-on. Medicine isn't always like that."

"You're right, but medicine offers a lot of variety. I'm hoping to be a doctor one day. I've completed my undergraduate work—I'll start medical school next fall."

"Really?"

Again the look of surprise. Well, she wouldn't be the first person to underestimate him. He enjoyed proving them wrong. "I've applied for some grants and scholarships," he said. "It won't be easy to pull everything together, but I'm determined."

"Why do you want to be a doctor?"

"The same reason you chose respiratory therapy, I guess. I want to help people."

Her expression softened. "That's really great."

She was really great. He couldn't believe she'd been here for months and he'd only just met her. "So this exchange program is for only one year?" he asked.

"Yes. My visa expires in January."

One more reason not to get too carried away with her, he told himself. But that didn't mean they couldn't enjoy the little time they had left together.

She finished stocking the cart and checked a computer printout. "I really do have to get back to work," she said.

"Sure. Well, see ya." He nodded, then turned and strode away, resisting the urge to whistle from sheer happiness.

WHEN ALINA WAS SURE Eric couldn't see her, she allowed herself to watch him as he walked away, a muscular, dark-haired man, all broad shoulders, slim hips and masculine energy. One of the aides almost collided with a doorjamb as she walked past him, and Alina knew the moment Eric smiled at the young woman by the dreamy expression that transformed her plain, weary face into one of beauty.

Resolutely Alina turned away and steered her cart toward her next patient—Mr. Herrera. The poor man was still in the hospital, not improving despite the best of care.

"Hello, Alina," Mrs. Herrera said, standing as Alina wheeled the cart into the room. "I'm so glad you're here. He's having such a hard time today and your breathing treatments always help so much."

"She's my angel," Mr. Herrera managed a weak smile between wheezing, tortured breaths.

"You should have called for me sooner," Alina scolded as she clipped on the pulse oxymeter and checked the reading. It was bad, though not life threatening.

"We didn't want to bother you," Mrs. Herrera said. "I looked out the door once, but I saw you were talking with your young man, and I didn't want to interrupt."

Alina felt her face burn, but she kept her voice casual. "He isn't my young man. You should have called me." Though she would have regretted the interruption. Why hadn't she met Eric earlier in the year? when they would have had more time to get to know each other?

"He was a handsome one." Mrs. Herrera smiled and squeezed her husband's hand. "He reminded me of Arturo when he and I first met."

Alina measured the medication into the nebulizer and handed the mouthpiece to Mr. Herrera. "Breathe as deeply as you can," she instructed. "But not too quickly. Try to relax."

He nodded and clamped his lips around the mouthpiece.

"What is your good-looking friend's name?" Mrs. Herrera asked.

"Eric. Eric Sepulveda."

"And what does he do?"

"He's a paramedic and a ski patroller. But he wants to be a doctor." She didn't know why she'd added this last bit, except that some part of her wanted Mrs. Herrera to be impressed with him. He'd surprised her with this glimpse of his ambitions. This revelation didn't fit with the picture Marissa had painted of the playboy ski patroller-paramedic who was never serious about anything, especially women.

"A doctor. That's very good."

Yes, Eric was a good man. Even *Baka* Fania, who doled out her approval like precious jewels, would have liked Eric.

She checked Mr. Herrera's pulse oxymeter. "You're doing great," she said. "Do you feel as if you're breathing easier?"

He nodded and squeezed her hand, his fingers bony, the skin stretched over them like dry silk. Mrs. Herrera held his other hand, stroking it over and over with the gentle touch of comfort and connection that went deeper than words. On an earlier visit, Alina had learned the two had been married fifty-two years.

"The first time we met, I wanted nothing to do with him," Mrs. Herrera had confided. "He had to win me over." She'd smiled. "I think it made him ap-preciate me more."

Oh, to be appreciated—loved—by one man for fifty-two years. That was the kind of happiness *Baka* Fania had predicted. The kind Alina was still searching for. She didn't care if the man she loved was blond, brunette or bald, as long as he was *the one* for her.

Chapter Four

Eric arrived at Alina's apartment Saturday morning with Marty and Marissa. All of them were dressed in ski pants and parkas, warm hats and gloves. Alina's hat was one *Baka* Fania had knitted before she died. Whenever she wore it, she felt her grandmother was closer to her. Though if *Baka* Fania were really here, she'd be pushing Alina toward Marty and away from Eric.

Sorry, Grandmother, Alina thought as she slid close to Eric in the front seat of the truck that pulled a trailer with two snowmobiles. *I guess I'm not attracted to blondes.*

They soon left Gunnison behind, headed toward Crested Butte. What had been a thin layer of snow on the ground became thicker drifts until, by the time they reached the top of Kebler Pass, the world looked iced in smooth white frosting, dark green firs and pines adorning it like Christmas decorations.

Another truck and trailer awaited them in the parking area near the top of the pass. "This is my friend Maddie, who works with me in the EMS, and her husband, Hagan, who heads up ski patrol." Eric made the introductions. "And these are my friends, Casey and Max Overbridge."

"Maddie and I have met at the hospital," Alina said. Maddie's husband, Hagan, looked like that gorgeous blond actor who'd played James Bond in the movies, while his friend Max was a big sandy-haired bear of a man.

The men set to work unloading the snowmobiles from the trailers while the women stood out of the way. Casey, with her cap of white-blond hair and delicate features, reminded Alina of the ballerina in a music box *Baka* Fania had once given her. "I visited Croatia once, about six years ago," Casey said. "I remember it was such a beautiful country."

"Oh? You came there on vacation?" Though more and more tourists arrived every year, Alina had met few Americans who had visited her homeland.

"Sort of," Casey said. "My dad is involved in politics in Chicago, and our whole family went on some kind of political junket. I spent most of my time avoiding official meetings, exploring the local markets and clubs. I met a lot of really nice people that way."

"Have you visited much of the United States while you've been here?" Maddie asked.

Alina shook her head. "I would like to see more of your country, but I have not had much time off work." When she did, she had no one to travel with, and little extra money to fund expeditions.

"The two of us went shopping in Denver," Marissa said. "And once we went off-roading in Ouray with friends."

"I wish I could say I've done more," Alina said. When

she'd first come to the United States she'd planned to have so many adventures. She'd wanted to travel and learn all kinds of new things. And of course, find the true love that had eluded her in Croatia. Time was running out to realize any of those goals.

"You still have a few months left," Casey said.

"You girls ready?" Max called, revving the engine on his snowmobile.

"Alina, you can ride with me," Eric said. "Marty will take Marissa."

Hagan and Maddie led the way, a rooster tail of snow shooting out behind them as they climbed the slope, the others in pursuit. "Hang on tight!" Eric called, then the snowmobile lurched forward.

The only thing Alina could hold on to was Eric. She grabbed for him, wrapping her arms around him as the snowmobiles raced up the steep incline. Her heart hammered wildly, partly from fear of being thrown off the roaring vehicle, partly from excitement. As a child she'd insisted on riding roller coasters at the amusement park, even though they terrified her. The combination of abject fear and adrenaline made her feel more alive than she did at any other time.

Eric revved the engine and they raced up ever-steeper slopes. Stifling a scream, Alina buried her face in the back of his jacket, the nylon smooth against her cheek, the sharp clean smell of snow mingled with the biting odor of exhaust and the more subtle masculine scent of Eric himself.

As the trail leveled out and the sound of the engine died to a low rumble, she noticed the hard muscles of his back and thighs pressed against hers and the expansion of his chest as he breathed in and out.

Gradually, trying not to call attention to herself, she eased her arms from around him and scooted back a little, though she kept her hands lightly on his waist to brace herself.

"You didn't have to move away," he said. "I kind of liked you holding on."

"I didn't want to squeeze the breath out of you."

"I wasn't having any trouble breathing."

Neither was she. They were both breathing hard, perhaps from more than the excitement of the climb.

They followed the others into the trees, down a narrow trail lined with boughs bent heavy with snow. "This is gorgeous," she said. "Like something out of a fairy tale." She wouldn't have been surprised if they'd rounded the corner and come upon a gingerbread cottage or an ice castle, complete with a wicked witch or a fur-clad wizard.

"I've seen deer and elk up here in the snow," Eric said. "Once I almost ran into a big porcupine, and another time I spotted a bobcat. There are mountain lions, too, though I've never seen anything but tracks."

Alina shivered. She had no desire to come face-to-face with a mountain lion. Though she enjoyed the outdoors, she'd been raised a city girl and didn't care to get *too* close to nature.

"There's something really cool I want to show you," Eric said. He turned off the main trail, away from the others.

"Where are we going?" Alina asked as the others disappeared from view.

"Just a little detour," Eric said. "We'll meet up with everyone else later, I promise."

She steadied herself against him, and bit back a protest. It wasn't as if she had anything to fear from Eric. He didn't strike her as the type to spirit her away to harm her, and the others wouldn't be far away.

But the thought of being alone with him made her nervous. Without other people around to provide a buffer, would he see how vulnerable she was to him? Would he realize how strongly she was attracted to him, in spite of her determination to keep things light and uncomplicated? She wanted to have fun with Eric, and to avoid a heartache when it came time for her to leave.

THE SNOWMOBILE GLIDED down a narrow trail through the trees. Though neither spoke, Eric was acutely aware of the woman riding behind him, her hands lightly clasping his hips, her body so close to his, though not quite touching. He was tempted to race the snowmobile again, so she'd be forced to hold on more tightly. But he didn't want to destroy the peace of this moment, the snow-draped woods silent and magical around them.

He slowed further as they rounded a curve, watching for the opening in the trees he remembered from previous explorations. It appeared suddenly, a gap marked by a snow-covered mound of tailings—rock debris dug from a mine.

He turned into the opening, and a cluster of ruined buildings loomed before them, wood weathered silver-gray, rusty metal roofs partially caved in or lying in pieces amid the drifts. Vacant doorways and windows gaped. He shut off the snowmobile and they removed their helmets.

Alina stared at the ruins. "Is it what you call a ghost town? Someone told me there are many of them in the American West."

"It's a little like that," Eric said. "This was an old silver mine, abandoned in the 1880s."

Alina climbed off the snowmobile and promptly sank to her knees in the snow.

"Sorry about that." He hauled her up onto firmer ground and held her for a moment, allowing her to steady herself.

Her eyes met his briefly, and her cheeks flushed. "Thank you," she murmured, and looked down, her lashes like dark lace against her creamy skin.

"Walk here under the trees or nearer the buildings," he said. "Where the snow isn't as thick."

They picked their way up to the cluster of buildings. Old cans and bottles and rusted-out pails testified to the lives of past occupants, while the remains of a campfire bore witness to more recent intrusions.

"The miners who settled in this area lived here year 'round," Eric said. "The only way to get to town in the winter was on snowshoes or skis."

"It must have been very cold." Alina shivered as she eyed the gaps in the log siding and the sloping dirt floors.

"I guess they thought all the suffering was worth it for the promise of getting rich," Eric said. "Though I don't think very many of them struck it big."

"I guess when you have a dream like that, it's hard to let go of it," Alina said.

"Especially when others were finding gold and silver," Eric said. "So they knew it was possible." He trailed a gloved hand along a hand-hewn doorpost, onto which some long-ago visitors had carved the letters *JK + MP.* "Kind of like me and my ambitions to become a doctor. It's a long shot, but I'm determined to make it happen."

"Your family must be very proud," Alina said.

"They are. But they worry, too," he said. "Not because they don't think I'm capable, but they know medical school is expensive and the work's hard. They don't want me to be disappointed. My mother especially doesn't want me to move away. She's tried to convince me to set my sights lower. She thinks being a paramedic should be enough."

"But it isn't." Alina nodded. "My parents didn't want me to come to the United States. They thought it was too far. Too dangerous."

"They didn't want you to be so far away from them," Eric said.

She nodded. "I hated to leave them, but at the same time, I felt I needed to get away." She glanced at him. "I wanted to find out what I could do on my own. And I thought maybe I needed to get out into the wider world to discover what I really wanted."

"And have you?" he asked.

"Sometimes I'm sure and then others…" She shook her head. "Sometimes I feel as if I'm standing still, waiting to see what will happen next."

"That's life, isn't it?" he asked. "Waiting to see what will happen?"

"I don't know. Some people seem much more active—making things happen instead of waiting for them."

"I guess the secret is knowing when to act and when to wait." Which was the best course to take with her? Did he tell her his feelings for her—how something had shifted inside of him the evening they'd met, so that he looked at life now through a lens colored by her? He couldn't explain why she made him feel so different, or how much that confused and even frightened him. But he wanted to be with her, to know her more and maybe, through her, discover more about himself.

It was a lot to expect of another person, the kind of expectation that might doom a relationship before it started. Better to keep his mouth shut and avoid scaring her off. He'd let her see he was interested and allow things to develop at her pace.

Of course, she might not return his feelings. Maybe he'd misread the interest in her eyes. The idea made his chest hurt. Still, he had to take the risk. The miners would have understood. Failure might lie ahead of him, but the hope he felt whenever he was near her compelled him to take the chance.

"Do you think if you had lived back then, you would have been a miner?" she asked.

"I don't know." He'd never given the question much thought. "Maybe."

"Marty said you were a risk-taker. That you race motorcycles and ski extreme terrain and crazy stuff like that."

"Do you think that's crazy?"

"It's dangerous. You could be killed."

He shrugged. "I could be killed crossing the street tomorrow. I try to be safe, not take stupid chances, and the thrill is worth it to me."

"I guess the miners felt the same way." She looked around them, at the collapsing buildings and the drifts of snow, not another person or building visible for miles. "It must have been very lonely up here, don't you think?" she said. "The miners didn't bring their wives and children with them, did they?"

"No. I think only the men lived up here. If they had families, they left them somewhere else. Maybe back east. This was pretty untamed country back then."

"I don't think it's very tame now, what with mountain lions and other wild animals running around."

He laughed. "That's the whole point of the National Forest and designated wilderness areas and such," he said. "To preserve a little of that wildness so that people like us can still experience it."

Her eyes met his, the directness of her gaze an unexpected reward after all her skittishness around him. "Thank you for bringing me here," she said. "Only this morning I was regretting that I haven't seen more of this country, and now I feel you've shown me something special in the present, and in the past."

Her words, so sweet and wistful, tugged at his heart. "You're welcome," he said, and took her hand. He thought she might resist, but she didn't. He wished they weren't both wearing gloves so he could feel her fingers warm in his.

"Tell me about Croatia," he said, as much to distract her and keep her from pulling away as to satisfy his curiosity about her country.

"What do you want to know?" she asked. "I don't think we have much mining there. It's a small country, but we have a little of everything—mountains and beautiful beaches on the Mediterranean."

"You mentioned your sisters are married. Do they live close?"

"Yes, they're both in Zagreb."

"And your grandparents? Are they still alive?"

She shook her head. "My mother's mother died two years ago. She lived with us while I was growing up."

"I bet you miss her."

"I do. She and I were close."

The sadness in her voice made him want to pull her to him and comfort her, but he held himself back, not wanting to push when she was beginning to let down her guard around him. "My grandmother isn't the kind of woman people get close to," he said. "Most people are a little afraid of her."

"Including you?" she sounded amused.

He laughed. "Including me. She fusses at me if she thinks I'm trying to charm her."

"Good for her. You charming men shouldn't always be allowed to get your way."

The teasing note in her voice filled him with lightness. He felt reckless and bold. They'd reached the end of the mine ruins and a thick grove of trees blocked their progress. They'd have to turn back, retrace their steps to the snowmobile and return to the others. If he was going to act, it had to be now.

"I guess we should go," she said. She started past him, but he put a hand on her arm to stop her.

"Not yet," he said. She'd labeled him a risk-taker; there was one more risk he intended to take. "Could you do me one favor?" he asked.

Her eyes were dark, wary, but he sensed no fear. "What is it?"

"Would you kiss me? Just once?"

He saw the impact of his words on her face, the shuttered look that came into her eyes, the almost imperceptible pulling away. Disappointment swelled his throat, choking off words. So much for thinking this attraction between them was anything but one-sided.

Then her eyelids fluttered shut and she leaned toward him, and pressed her lips to his, a soft, sweet offering that rocked him back on his heels.

He put out a hand to steady himself and she leaned into him farther, a sigh escaping her, emboldening him to slip his arms around her and pull her closer. She didn't resist, but softened in his arms, cuddling against him, her body molded to his, her lips parted slightly in invitation.

An invitation he gladly accepted, deepening the kiss, losing himself in the scent and touch and taste of her. She arched against him, her gloved fingertips caressing the back of his neck. The tenderness of the gesture sent a shudder through him as if she'd reached out to some hidden part of him, rendering him as vulnerable as if she'd stripped him naked.

The idea shook him so that he was the first to pull away, struggling to regain his equilibrium and sense of self. They each took a step back and made a show of straightening their clothing, stealing glances at each other, the intensity of the encounter rendering them too shy to speak. She squeezed his hand once, then moved past him, back down the path toward the snowmobile.

ALINA LEANED against Eric's back as he guided the snowmobile back the way they'd come. She was reluctant to let go of the heat that had filled her when their lips met, wishing she could keep the feeling like a souvenir. She'd tuck it into the ballerina music box, next to the pressed flowers she'd worn in her hair at Zora's wedding and the postcard from her trip to Dubrovnik when she was twelve.

She should have been shocked when Eric asked to kiss her, but as soon as he uttered the words, she realized she'd been waiting for them. They'd been almost inevitable as soon as she'd accepted his invitation to come with him today, and once he'd turned away from the others she'd known this moment would come with all the certainty with which *Baka* Fania had foretold her sisters' marriages or the location of her aunt Oksana's lost diamond ring.

Baka Fania had believed strongly that everything happened for a reason. Using that logic, Alina was meant to kiss Eric. He couldn't be her forever lover, but maybe he had some lesson to teach her or message to impart.

Or could she just be rationalizing everything? She certainly hadn't kissed Eric like a woman who thought of him only as a casual friend. She'd put heart and soul into that kiss; not because she'd set out to do so, but because she'd been helpless to respond to him in any other way. Something in him called to her in a primitive way that went beyond conversation and deeper than surface emotion or logic.

Now she felt branded by that kiss, destined to compare every other to it for the rest of her life.

"What were you two doing off by yourselves?" Marissa teased when Alina and Eric rejoined the rest of the group. They'd all stopped by the side of a frozen creek to eat lunch.

"We visited some old mine ruins," Alina said, avoiding looking at her friend directly.

"Sure you did. And your lips are only swollen from the wind."

Alina put a hand to her lips. They didn't feel swollen to her. She realized her mistake when Marissa laughed. "Gotcha!" her friend said, and darted out of reach of Alina's ill-aimed blow.

While Hagan built a campfire, Eric and Max unpacked thermoses of chili and packets of ham sandwiches from backpacks. Alina accepted a sandwich and a mug of chili, then looked for a place to sit around the campfire.

"There's space on this log next to me," Marty said, but he said it like a man who was offering space to any casual acquaintance, not as if he was flirting with her or anything.

Alina glanced toward Eric, who was busy adding wood to the fire. Not wanting to be rude to Marty, she reluctantly made herself as comfortable as possible next to him on the cold log, legs stretched in front of her, sandwich balanced on one knee. "Where did you and Marissa and the others go while Eric and I were looking at the mine ruins?" she asked.

"We followed the creek for a while," Marty said.

"There are a couple of places where it isn't frozen over yet. We saw some tracks Max thinks belonged to a fox, but we never saw the fox."

"Have you spent much time outdoors?" she asked. "Do you ski or ride mountain bikes?"

"Not much." He shrugged. "I'm not much of an athlete. I ski a little, and I like to watch football. I played a little in high school, but that's about it."

Alina didn't consider herself an athlete, but the area around Crested Butte and Gunnison offered so many opportunities to enjoy being out of doors it seemed a shame not to take advantage of them. "Why did you decide to become a minister?" she asked.

"Well, my father is a pastor, so I grew up in that life. I always thought it was something I wanted to do. Some people talk about a calling, but it's not as if I was struck with a divine revelation or anything. It just seemed like something I'd enjoy and I'd be good at."

He sounded so calm and practical. She thought of Eric and his determination to become a doctor, despite the time and effort and great expense required.

"Somebody needs to tell a story," Marissa said. "Isn't that what you're supposed to do around a campfire?"

"I have a story to tell," Hagan volunteered in heavily accented English. "About Eric."

"Hagan, no!" Eric protested.

"You don't even know what I will say yet."

"I don't have to. If you're telling it, it must not be something good."

"Now you have to tell us," Marissa said. "We're dying to know."

"This happened last ski season, one day when Eric and I were both working patrol." Hagan leaned forward, elbows on his knees, blue eyes sparkling with barely repressed mirth. "A very large man and his wife decided to ski the extreme area off of Teocalli Bowl."

"Hagan, don't tell that story," Eric protested.

"The couple were not really skilled enough for the terrain," Hagan continued. "But the man had been drinking and boasted he could do it. He skied into the trees and lost his balance in the thick powder, then twisted his knee and was too out of shape to pull himself up."

"What about his wife?" Casey asked.

"She saw her husband fall and was smart enough to take off her skis and walk down to him," Hagan said. "She flagged down help, and Eric took the call."

"I should have made you go," Eric said. "The guy was huge. I didn't see how I was ever going to get him off the mountain on a sled."

"The terrain was too steep for a snowmobile," Hagan said. "In training in that area, we'd worked on winching a Stokes basket back up the slope to the top to a trail the snowmobile could navigate."

"Which takes forever," Eric argued. "Not to mention we have to shut down that whole area while we work and everybody risks back strain trying to haul up the big sucker."

"I am telling this story," Hagan said.

"What happened?" Marissa asked.

"I was seriously tempted to drag him to a clear spot and let him roll down the mountain," Eric said, ignoring Hagan's glare. "He had enough antifreeze in him he probably wouldn't even have noticed. He'd have showed up at the bottom as a big snow log."

"But you didn't do that," Marissa said.

"No, I didn't do that," Eric said.

"Instead, Eric decided he could ski down with the guy on his own," Hagan said. "So he put him in the basket."

"I had to roll him in like a beached whale," Eric said. "The guy was total deadweight and his wife fluttered around half-hysterical. She was no help at all. I finally sent her down ahead of us and told her to wait at the aid station."

"That was his only smart move," Hagan said. "He left the rest of his brains at home that day."

"Uh-oh," Casey said.

"Yes, uh-oh," Hagan said. "He stood to step into his skis and slipped."

"I guess I kicked the sled," Eric said. "It swung around perpendicular to the slope and took off."

"I looked up and this unmanned rescue sled was hurtling down the slope," Hagan said. "It was going much too fast."

"When I saw it, my whole future flashed before my eyes," Eric said. "Gravity had this big guy flying easily forty miles an hour. I was certain he was going to crash and burn over the side of a cliff. I'd have felt terrible if the guy got seriously hurt, not to mention I'd be paying off the lawsuit for the rest of my life."

"Fortunately the man in the sled had no idea," Hagan said. "He was wrapped up and couldn't see a thing. The sled sped past me to the bottom of the slope, managing to miss every tree on the way. At the bottom it skid into a big soft snowdrift."

"I hightailed it down there, dug the guy out and skied to the first-aid station as if nothing had ever happened," Eric said. "Then I went and threw up."

"The wife was thrilled Eric had brought her husband down so quickly," Hagan said. "The next day she presented him with a big bottle of fancy Scotch."

"That's amazing," Marissa said, laughing.

"He leads a charmed life," Hagan concluded. "Even his mistakes work out well in the end."

Alina glanced at Eric, who was laughing along with everyone else. At that moment, his eyes met hers and she felt again the strong pull of attraction between them. He had the power to make her feel as out of control as that man who had hurtled down the slope. She only hoped she'd come out of this as safe and unharmed.

Chapter Five

Alina called her parents every Monday afternoon to hear their news and share a little bit of her life in the States. She sent them photographs and gifts they couldn't get in Croatia, such as peanut butter cookies and buffalo jerky. She had given up inviting them to visit her; they always protested the expense was too great and the distance too far, so she was startled when they broke this routine the last week of October.

"Alina, this is your mama," her mother announced when Alina answered the telephone as she was getting ready for work one morning. As if anyone else would call at this hour and speak to her in Croatian.

"Mama, is everything all right?" Alina's heart raced. "Is Papa—?"

"Papa is fine. I'm calling to wish you happy birthday. *Sretan rodendan!*"

"Aw, Mama, thank you!" A lump rose in Alina's throat. She'd avoided thinking about her birthday this year. She didn't feel she had much to celebrate, being so far from her parents and further still from the kind of life she wanted to lead, with a home and family of her own.

"We have another surprise for you," her mother continued. "We are coming to visit you next month."

"You are?" Alina sat down hard on the side of her bed. "I mean, that's wonderful. What changed your mind?"

"Your cousin Valentina said she could get us tickets." Free tickets, Alina assumed, since her cousin worked for an airline. Yet how many times had Alina offered to pay for her parents to visit? Of course, in that case Alina would be spending *her* money, which her parents would think was almost as bad as them spending their own.

"Your father read a newspaper article about the American Thanksgiving and thought that would be good to see," her mother continued. Translation: coming such a long way to visit family was too frivolous for her father, a professor, but if he could research some interesting American social custom, he could justify the time and effort.

"That's terrific." Alina scanned the hospital schedule tacked to her kitchen wall. "So you're arriving when? And staying through the fourth weekend in November?"

"We're arriving the twelfth of November and staying until December first."

"Wonderful." Alina looked around her small apartment. She'd have three weeks to rearrange her schedule at the hospital and the furniture to accommodate her parents. "I can't wait." Already some of her surprise was fading, replaced by anticipation and a longing to see them.

"You must tell me what to pack," her mother said. "Is it very cold there now? And I'll bring you some *ajvar* and that good chocolate you love. I know you can't get them in the United States. And I should bring candied figs for your father. He gets very grouchy when he doesn't have them."

Alina smiled at the image of her parents standing in the airport, surrounded by a mountain of luggage, like emigrants determined to bring everything they owned with them. "Bring yourselves, that's all I want," she said. She could think of no better birthday gift than to know that her family would soon be here with her.

She carried her excitement with her to the hospital, where Marissa was just finishing her shift. "You're looking perky this morning," Marissa said.

At Alina's puzzled look, Marissa explained, "*Perky* means energetic. Bubbly."

Alina nodded. "My parents are coming to visit. In three weeks. My mother called this morning with the news."

"That's wonderful. They'll be here for Thanksgiving?"

"Yes. They want to see the American holiday."

"Oh. I never thought about it, but I guess you don't have Thanksgiving in Croatia."

"No. And my dad's a sociology professor at the University of Zagreb. He loves to study any kind of social custom. Knowing him, he'll have a paper half written before he leaves here."

"No wonder you're so smart. I can't wait to meet your folks."

Alina read through the various notices in her in-box. "Anything interesting happen during your shift?"

"Not really. But you'll be happy to hear Mr. Herrera is being discharged this morning."

"That's wonderful. So he's doing better?"

Marissa made a face. "He's stable. I guess that's the best the poor dear can hope for at this stage." Marissa gave her a hug. "I have to run now. Talk to you later."

After Marissa had left, Alina hurried to Mr. Herrera's room to say goodbye. She found Mrs. Herrera struggling to carry a large arrangement of flowers and a battered suitcase. "Let me help you with those," Alina said, rushing to take the flowers. She looked around the blossoms to Mr. Herrera, who waited in a wheelchair by the door. "I imagine you are glad to be going home today, no?" she asked.

"It'll be good to sleep in my own bed again." He held out a trembling hand. "I'll miss seeing you, dear."

"I'll miss you, too." She gave his hand a gentle squeeze, wishing she could throw her arms around him and hug him hard, the way she had her *Baka* Fania. But rules of professionalism forbid such overly physical demonstrations of affection.

"A home health aide is supposed to come out every day to check on him," Mrs. Herrera said. "I know how to give him his breathing treatments, but I still worry."

"If you have any questions at all, you call his doctor right away," Alina said. "And try not to worry too much."

Mrs. Herrera shrugged. "After more than fifty years, I think it's a habit. I wouldn't know what to do with myself without this old man to fuss over." The tender look she gave her husband belied the sternness of her words.

Alina escorted the old couple to a waiting taxi and waved until they were out of sight. She'd miss seeing them, but she hoped it would be a long time before Mr.

Herrera had to return to the hospital. Such a devoted couple deserved many more happy years together.

The rest of the day passed uneventfully. At lunch, she treated herself to a slice of chocolate cake and said a silent "Happy Birthday." Turning twenty-seven by herself wasn't so bad after all. She might not have a husband and children yet, but she had loving parents and friends, a job she found rewarding and a lifetime of opportunities ahead of her. The best was yet to come, though she wouldn't mind if her dreams came true sooner rather than later.

At six, as she was preparing to end her shift, she was surprised to see Marissa again. "Are you working a split shift today?" Alina asked.

"No, silly, I came to take you out for your birthday."

Alina flushed. "How did you know it was my birthday?" She had been careful to keep the day a secret, not wanting anyone to make a fuss.

"A woman in human resources is a friend of mine and she looked it up for me. You didn't think you could keep a secret like that from me, did you?"

Alina hugged her friend. "Thank you for going to all that trouble," she said. "It did feel strange today not celebrating."

"Well, we're going to celebrate now." Marissa held out a shopping bag. "Starting with this. Change out of those scrubs and into some party clothes."

"What is this?" Alina asked, looking into the bag.

"Just some things I pulled together. Now, hurry up. We have places to be and people to see."

A true fashionista, Marissa had chosen an outfit Alina

would never have bought for herself, but one she had to admit looked great on her: skinny black leggings and a bright, fluttery tunic that hugged her curves and showed off a little cleavage. "I can't let my mother see this," Alina said when she emerged from the employee locker room.

"Your mother isn't here." She grabbed Alina's hand. "Come on. Let's go."

The friends headed out of town, toward Crested Butte. Marissa's lime-green Volkswagen Beetle hugged the curves along the river, past barren fields where scattered deer grazed. Most of the snow from the last storm had melted, though the mountains ahead would remain frosted white until well into summer.

Marissa slowed the car as they neared downtown Crested Butte. They passed the shining silver dragon sculpture that marked the entrance to town, and turned left at the Chamber of Commerce office onto Elk Avenue. Some of the shop windows were decorated for Halloween with skeletons and pumpkins while others sported scarecrows and cornucopias. Most of the year the sidewalks and the bright Victorian buildings lining the street were filled with tourists enjoying the winter snow, fall foliage or summer wildflowers. But in these few weeks after the first light snows and before the opening of the ski resort the streets were mostly empty.

"Where are we going?" Alina asked.

"You'll see." Marissa pulled the car to the curb at the end of the block. "Come on," she said as she switched off the engine. "Everybody's waiting."

Heart fluttering as wildly as the multicolored skirts of her tunic, Alina followed her friend up a flight of

wooden steps at the back of a pale blue building with
yellow eaves and shutters. "You go first," Marissa said,
and urged Alina ahead of her through the open door.

"Surprise!" Everything happened exactly the way
Alina had seen it in the movies: cameras flashed, con-
fetti showered down and a dozen people crowded
around to hug her and wish her a happy birthday. Casey
and Max, Maddie and Hagan, and Marty were all there,
along with a few people she didn't know.

Eric was the last to greet her. "Happy birthday,
Alina," he said, and enveloped her in a hug.

The instant his arms encircled her, she was transported
back to that clearing in the snow and that incredible kiss.
Only the crowd around them prevented her from giving
in to the urge to repeat the experience. She settled instead
for returning the hug and smiling up at him. "Thank you.
It's turning out to be a wonderful birthday."

She couldn't believe everyone had gone to so much
trouble for her. She felt so welcomed and embraced.
This is the way life had been when she was a little girl,
when her neighborhood was a small town. Everyone
knew everyone. People came every day to consult *Baka*
Fania about their futures. She always gave good advice
and never accepted payment, though she would allow
her patrons to make gifts to Alina's mother of the pepper
and honey biscuits called *Paprenjak* that *Baka* Fania
adored, or the candied figs her father preferred. Alina
missed that lifestyle almost as much as she missed her
grandmother.

"Okay, everybody, time to serenade the birthday
girl!" Zephyr, a lanky man with blond dreadlocks, stood

on a coffee table and strummed an electric guitar. "Happy, happy, happy birthday to you!" he sang, gesturing for the others to join in. "Happy, happy, happy birthday to you! Happy, happy, happy, birthday to you! We wish you all a great day and better year, too."

ERIC WATCHED Alina's reaction to Zephyr's birthday serenade. Locals took the eccentric rocker for granted; it was fun to see him through a newcomer's eyes. She stared, a half smile on her lips, as if unsure how to react. Eric moved over beside her. "Zephyr's lyrics aren't always the greatest, but he makes up for them with enthusiasm," he said.

She nodded. Head down, arms akimbo and dreadlocks flying, Zephyr strummed furiously at the guitar. His birthday song morphed into a lively number.

"Want to dance?" Eric asked.

"Sure."

Eric would have preferred a slow dance and the chance to hold Alina in his arms. He had so many things he wanted to say to her—about the kiss they'd shared, about the closeness he felt to her even though they'd known each other such a short time—but the opportunity for such confidences hadn't presented itself.

He thought he might say something when their dance ended, but they were interrupted once more. "Pizza's here!" Max entered the room, his arms stacked with pizza boxes.

Zephyr stopped playing midsong. "All right, I'm starved!"

"Do they have pizza in Croatia?" Eric asked Alina

after they'd helped themselves to their share of the pepperoni pies.

"We have very good pizza in Croatia," she said. "We have great seafood and sausage and wonderful baked goods, too." She picked a slice of pepperoni from her pizza and nibbled it. "Food always tastes better when it's eaten with friends, no?"

"No. I mean, yes." Though he could have been eating sawdust for all he knew right now—his senses were too focused on Alina to register anything else.

He thought he might find the opportunity to speak with her alone after they finished eating, but once again he was thwarted.

"Come over here, birthday girl," Marissa said as soon as they were done. "Come look at all your gifts." She dragged a protesting Alina away.

Eric found a seat on a sofa and after a few minutes, Marty joined him. The big blond had a plate piled high with pizza, and wore a purple conical party hat on his head—the kind designed for children, so it was too small.

"What's with the hat?" Eric asked.

Marty grinned. "Marissa gave it to me when I came in the door. Told me I had to wear it. How did she miss you?"

"Guess I'm just lucky."

"Nice party," Marty said. "I think Alina's having a good time."

Eric's gaze settled on Alina once more. She wore a sparkling tiara and a necklace of silk flowers. Marissa said something that made her laugh, then Alina twirled, the skirts of her tunic belling out around her. She looked so young and carefree and beautiful, like an exotic butterfly.

"You know if you keep looking at her that way, you're liable to melt something," Marty said.

"Looking at her what way?" Eric forced his gaze away from the women.

"Like a lovesick dog." Marty chuckled. "Why don't you just put yourself out of your misery and ask her out on a real date? And don't give me all that bull about not upsetting your mother and your grandmother. That's just an excuse."

Maybe Marty was right. Eric had let the conversation with his brothers at the barbecue shake him up too much. After all, he'd dated girls before—girls his family would have considered even more unsuitable than Alina—and that hadn't triggered any alarm bells. He probably had several carefree years in front of him before his mother and grandmother really started getting desperate. By then he'd have completed school and his medical training and be ready to settle down anyway.

"Maybe I will ask her out," he said. But he'd wait until she wasn't surrounded by her girlfriends, who'd probably figure out what he was up to and let the whole town know about it.

"Alina's going to open her gifts now." Marissa clapped her hands and waited for the crowd to quiet.

Blushing prettily, Alina settled into a blue rocking chair and accepted the first wrapped package. "First, I want to thank you all so much," she said. "I never had such a fun party in my life."

She smiled at everyone, but Eric responded as if the look was for him alone, his heart feeling too big for his chest.

The first gift was from Zephyr and his girlfriend, Trish—a bag of coffee beans from Trish's coffee shop. "I wanted to give you this really cool stuffed moose head I found at a tag sale," Zephyr said, "but Trish convinced me the coffee beans would be easier to carry back to Croatia. Or you could just brew them all before then."

"Thank you," Alina said. "And thank you to Trish, also."

Other packages revealed a Ski Patrol T-shirt from Hagan and Maddie, chocolates from Casey and Max, and a book about Colorado wildflowers from Marty.

Alina opened Eric's gift last. She held up the thin gold chain from which dangled an aspen leaf charm. "It's a real aspen leaf," he explained. "Encased in some kind of resin. Now you can take a little bit of Colorado with you wherever you go."

"It's beautiful," she said. "Thank you so much."

"But wait, there's more!" Zephyr exclaimed as Maddie and Marissa carried out a cake blazing with candles.

Alina's eyes widened. "This is too much!" she protested.

"Quick, make a wish and blow out all the candles," Marissa said.

So Alina sucked in a deep breath and blew out the candles while everyone applauded.

As the others crowded around the cake, Alina excused herself. Eric saw her slip out a side door, and he followed her.

The door opened onto a little balcony that looked out onto the street and the mountains beyond. Alina stood at the railing, staring out at the view. "Are you okay?" he asked.

She turned to him, smiling. "I'm good. Everything is so wonderful I wanted to come out here and savor it. I don't like it when good things go by too fast."

"Let me guess—when you were a little girl, you hoarded your Christmas candy and rationed it out instead of eating it all at once."

She laughed. "How did you know?"

"Just a guess." He came to stand beside her at the balcony railing. "I ate mine all at once."

"Because you wanted to enjoy it all then?" she asked.

"Partly. And maybe partly because I always knew there'd be more." He glanced at her. "If you haven't already figured it out, as the baby of the family, I was a little bit spoiled."

"I was the baby, too," she said. "I never thought of myself as spoiled, just well loved."

Love. The word made his throat constrict. He couldn't say if that was what he felt for Alina. It seemed too soon for such strong emotion.

All he knew was that she made him feel like no other woman had. Now, when they were alone, was the perfect opportunity to tell her. But his tongue was tied. What if she thought he was a nut, coming on too strong? What if she told him she didn't want anything to do with him anymore?

Other people labeled him a risk-taker because he liked the adrenaline rush of extreme sports and relished the thrill of trying new things, but no risk he'd confronted before had been as daunting as being honest about his feelings for this woman.

"I want to see you again," he blurted.

"You're seeing me right now," she said, her voice perfectly even.

English wasn't her first language, but he was sure she knew the meaning behind his words. Was she trying to put him off politely, or merely making him work to win her? Women could be perverse that way. "I want to date you," he said.

A tiny, perfect V creased her forehead as she studied him. "You know I have to go back to Croatia in the middle of January," she said.

The reminder sent a stab of pain through his chest. "We've got almost three months until then," he said.

"So, we go out for three months, and then I leave?"

Did she have to state things so bluntly? He much preferred to pretend January would never get here. Though, given his own plans, a relationship with a guaranteed expiration date was the only kind he could afford to have. "We could have a lot of fun in that time," he said. "You could go home with some good memories."

"So you're promising me good memories?" Her eyes sparkled with amusement, teasing him.

He leaned closer, and put his hand at her waist. "We could make some very good memories," he whispered.

He'd already made one bold move, asking her out, so he decided to build on that and risk another kiss. She made a sound in the back of her throat he worried was a protest, then she rested her hand against his cheek and leaned into him.

"I think I could enjoy kissing you for the next three months," she murmured.

"Anything for the birthday girl," he said, and kissed her again. He wouldn't think about their future, or lack of one, right now. The best experiences should always be lived in the moment, whether it was skiing a challenging slope, racing a tough course or romancing a beautiful woman like Alina.

Chapter Six

For their first official date, Eric asked Alina to go hiking with him. On a cold, clear Saturday in late October they drove to a trailhead in the mountains and set out. Alina was glad he'd chosen an activity that would keep them moving—not because she was that much of an athlete, but because it allowed for more conversation than a movie date and felt less intimate than dinner in a restaurant.

As much as she told herself this was just another date, like dozens she'd had before, being with Eric felt different. More dangerous to her emotional equilibrium. As she hiked behind him on the narrow trail, she couldn't help imagining *Baka* Fania was shaking her head in disapproval. Why was Alina wasting time with the wrong man when she should be out looking for the one her grandmother had predicted would make her happy?

Eric makes me happy for now, she would have told her grandmother.

She wished *Baka* Fania was here to talk to. Alina would ask her grandmother what was in store for her once she returned to Croatia. Would she find happiness there? Did happiness really depend on the blond man who had so far eluded her?

Or maybe there was no blond man. Alina had always been so close to her grandmother. Maybe that closeness prevented the older woman from seeing the younger woman's future clearly.

The trail was steep, and Alina had a hard enough time breathing, much less talking, so she and Eric said little for the first hour of their hike.

Eric paused at the top of a switchback and waited for her to catch up. "Am I going too fast?" he asked.

"No…I'm just…still not used…to the altitude," she panted.

"It gets a little easier from here," he said. "Not as steep. I've skied this area in the winter."

She looked down the way they'd come, at what seemed almost a sheer drop. A thin layer of snow covered the ground, though dark brown earth and the yellow of fallen aspen leaves broke up the white expanse. "Do you really ski something so difficult?" she asked.

"You bet. It's a blast."

"Why do you do it?"

"I don't know." He paused as if trying to find the right words. "I guess to prove to myself I can," he said after a moment. "To conquer my fears. When you do something like that—something that scares you, that has an element of danger—there's an incredible adrenaline rush. For a while you feel invincible."

She stared at the slope again and shuddered. "I guess I'm not much of a risk-taker."

"You took a risk coming to America by yourself, didn't you?" he said. "That must have been scary."

"A little. But it didn't feel like a very big deal. My life in Croatia had gotten stale. I needed a change, and this was a good opportunity."

"What will you do when you go back?"

"I don't know." She didn't like to think about it. What waited for her there but more of the dullness she'd come here to escape?

"Do you like it here?" he asked. "Would you stay if you could?"

"Yes. I've thought about applying for a different kind of visa, but the rules are very strict."

"Maybe you could arrange a green card marriage." His laugh sounded forced.

"It doesn't work that way anymore," she said. "The rules are much more stringent since September 11."

"Damn. I was going to offer to be your green card groom."

He looked away from her as he spoke, staring across the valley below, so that she couldn't read the expression in his eyes. Of course he was joking, she told herself, though the fluttering in her chest didn't feel like laughter. "Now you are safe," she said.

"Yes." He turned and started up the trail again, and she followed. "I ought to get through medical school before I marry anyway," he called over his shoulder. "That and a residency and then internships would be hard on a marriage."

"Yes. But people do it."

"I guess some of them do. It would be hard, though."

Harder than skiing this steep terrain? Harder than getting into medical school in the first place?

They fell silent, breathing heavily as they scaled an even steeper slope. So much for him telling her the climbing got easier. "My parents are coming to visit," she said when the path flattened out and she could catch her breath. "For Thanksgiving."

"That's great. Have they been to the U.S. before?"

"No. I'm excited to see them. And a little worried, too."

"Oh? Why?"

"I've been on my own for a while now. I'm used to living by myself, doing as I please. I'm afraid my parents will have much to say about how I should live my life. In my country parents, especially those of single women, feel they have that right."

"Do what I do," he said. "Listen and nod and agree with everything they say, then do what you want anyway."

She drew alongside him. "Is that what you do?"

He laughed. "Sometimes. Don't get me wrong. I really respect my parents."

"They seem very nice." She remembered how they had welcomed her to their barbecue and had obviously done well in raising Eric.

"They're pretty amazing people," he said. "My dad came to this country from Mexico when he was seven. His parents were migrant workers. My mom was born in Gunnison, but her parents were immigrants. They both worked really hard to make a good life. My dad's a real leader in the community. His machine shop employs a lot of family and friends, and he coaches youth soccer. My mother is on the altar guild at church and was really involved when we were in school."

"I guess they've worked so hard to raise you, they want to see you have a good life."

"Yeah. Whenever I get tired of them telling me what to do, I remind myself that I could probably learn a few things from them about being happy and successful."

"Yes, but maybe sometimes we have different ideas from them about what would make us happy." For her parents, happiness was living in their little apartment in the city, keeping the old traditions, their children all close to home. Alina was restless for more. She craved a husband and children of her own, but she didn't think her home or her life would be like her parents'. She cherished the old traditions, but wanted to make new ones, as well.

She brushed something cold from her face. Looking down at her arms, she saw white flecks against the red of her jacket. "I think it's snowing," she said.

Eric tilted his head back and studied the sky. Though the sun still shone, dark clouds were moving in. "I think you're right," he said. "Snow wasn't predicted for today, but the weather can change here pretty quickly. We'd better head back."

By the time they descended to treeline, it was snowing hard. Eric took her hand in his. "If the visibility gets bad, I don't want us separated," he said.

At first she thought he was overreacting—or using this as an excuse to hold hands—but as snow swirled around them and it became harder and harder to see, she was grateful for his hand holding firmly to hers.

They stumbled blindly down what she hoped was the trail. "How can you see where you're going?" she asked.

"I can see a little, and I can still make out some landmarks."

"Maybe we should stop," she said.

"We'd have to build a shelter. And it's going to be dark soon. We'd have to spend the night out here."

She shuddered. The thought of spending the night in the cold and darkness frightened her. "I guess we should go on."

"As long as I can see, I think we should," he said. "The trailhead isn't that far."

She remembered all the stories she'd read in the paper about people who got lost in the mountains of Colorado. They fell off cliffs or wandered for days in the wilderness or froze to death within yards of the correct trail. She squeezed Eric's hand harder. "If you're sure."

He stopped and faced her. "If it gets much worse, I promise we'll stop," he said. "I've got some emergency supplies in my pack, and I've had wilderness survival training, so we should be fine. I'd never do anything to put you in danger."

She saw no fear in his eyes, only reassurance. She nodded. "I know that." She forced a smile. "If I had to get caught in a snowstorm, I guess I'm lucky to be with a trained professional."

He patted her shoulder. "That's right. Now let's get going."

They half ran, half slid down the path. She kept her head down, trying to watch where she was going, trusting Eric to guide her, his hand securely clutching hers.

Despite the blinding snow and perilous conditions, she felt safe and warm in his grasp.

Snow lay thick on the ground by the time they reached the trailhead, the bright red of his truck barely visible through the swirling white. They stumbled to the vehicle, and Alina shook with cold and relief as she waited for Eric to unlock the doors.

"I'm sorry for getting us into this situation," he said once they were safely inside the cab. "I should have kept a closer eye on the weather."

"No, no. It's not your fault. You're my hero for getting us back safely." She was sure she never would have made it alone, yet he had never panicked. She leaned over and threw her arms around him and gave him a quick kiss. His lips were cold, and she realized he was shivering also.

"We'd better get somewhere warm," he said, and started the truck.

They drove in silence toward town, in swirling snow. Alina felt as if she was suspended inside a souvenir snow globe. This one would have mountains and a banner that said Experience the Romance of Crested Butte.

They passed no other vehicles and saw no one else on the road; they might have been the only people who existed in this magical world of white. Now that her fear had subsided and her hands and feet had thawed, Alina saw the good side of the afternoon's events. She felt closer to Eric now, drawn by the intimacy of shared danger safely past.

"I still can't believe you managed to stay on the trail and lead us to the truck," she said.

"I have good instincts," he said. "And a strong sense of self-preservation."

"Good qualities for a ski patroller and an EMT," she said. The kind of man any woman could rely on. Though Alina was a modern woman who believed in her ability to stand on her own feet, she couldn't deny the attraction of a man who was strong enough to let her lean on him, if she ever needed to do so.

The town of Crested Butte looked deserted, the lights of stores and houses glowing dimly through the snow. "Has everyone gone home?" Alina asked.

"Not everyone." He parked in front of Trish's coffee shop.

Inside, they found Zephyr and Trish at one of the little tables. "I was just debating closing up and going home," Trish said. She stood. "What can I get for you two?"

"Hot chocolate," Eric said. He glanced at Alina. "What about you?"

"Hot chocolate sounds good." She shed her hat, gloves and jacket and dropped into a chair.

"You look frozen," Zephyr said.

"We were hiking and got caught in the storm," Eric said.

"You really know how to impress the ladies," Zephyr said. "Take them into the mountains and let 'em almost freeze to death."

Though she knew Zephyr was only teasing, Alina didn't like this implied criticism of Eric. She searched for some way to tactfully change the subject and spotted the giant paper spider that hung from the shop ceiling. "I see you are decorated for Halloween," she said.

"It's my favorite holiday," Zephyr said.

"Not that people around here need much of an excuse to dress up in crazy costumes," Trish said. "But we do have a lot of fun with it."

"Most people in Croatia don't celebrate Halloween," Alina said. "Until maybe ten years ago, no one had really heard of it. Now television will show scary movies on the thirty-first of October, and some people have parties, but it's considered an American holiday."

"We always decorate, and when I was a kid we looked forward to trick-or-treating," Eric said. "But in my family, the really big day is the day after Halloween."

"Why is that?" Trish asked.

"November first is *Dia de los Muertos,*" he said. "Day of the Dead. Some people know it as All Saints Day. It's a day to honor deceased relatives, but at our house it always means a big party with candy skulls and special food."

"Candy skulls?" Zephyr's eyes widened. "Radical!"

"We don't have anything like that in Croatia," Alina said.

"You should come to the party," Eric said.

"Are you sure it would be all right?" she asked. "Isn't it for family?"

"Family and friends. Last year Marty came. He'll probably come this year, too."

If nothing else, going to this party would be a way for her to honor the memory of her grandmother. "All right," she said. "Thank you for inviting me."

"Bring me back a sugar skull," Zephyr said.

ALINA SPENT Halloween at the hospital, a pair of kitten ears, painted-on whiskers and a long tail tacked onto the back of her scrubs serving as her costume. Her co-workers roamed the halls as witches, vampires, pumpkins, clowns, various animals from apes to a pig, scarecrows and dozens of other creative disguises.

"What did you do this weekend?" Marissa, dressed as a rag doll in a red yarn wig, red-and-white-striped tights and a ruffled dress, asked Alina as they shared a lunch of turkey wraps and pumpkin cookies from the hospital cafeteria.

"I went hiking," she said, biting back a smile.

"With whom?" Marissa's eyes sparkled. "Or can't I guess?"

Alina allowed the smile to show.

"It was Eric, wasn't it?" Marissa laughed. "Is that all you did—hike?"

"It started to snow, so we came back to Crested Butte and had hot chocolate." Maybe that didn't sound terribly romantic to Marissa, but Alina could think of few better ways to spend a snowy afternoon.

"You two are really into each other, aren't you?" Marissa said.

"Into each other?" Alina frowned, trying to decipher the idiom.

"I mean, you really like each other, even though you haven't known each other very long."

"I like him." The words didn't seem enough to explain all she felt for Eric.

"So maybe this is serious?" Marissa asked.

"Serious?"

"I know your English is better than that. You know what I mean. Are you in love?"

The word was like a tiny shock of electricity applied directly to her heart. "Eric and I are friends," she protested, even as a voice inside her whispered that that wasn't the whole truth. She felt things for Eric she had never felt for another man—a contentment and confidence when she was with him she'd never known before, a closeness that went beyond someone she'd only spent a few hours with. But how could she call that love? It was impossible.

"Friendship can lead to love," Marissa observed. "From the little I've seen you two together, I'd say it's a definite possibility in your case."

Alina looked away. "We're just friends." She was leaving soon; she couldn't afford for them to mean more to each other.

"He's a great guy," Marissa said. "I think the two of you are perfect for each other."

Alina shook her head. "He's not interested in getting serious about anyone. Not for years. He told me himself he wants to finish medical school and training before he marries."

"People have been known to change their minds about that kind of thing when the right person comes along."

"I don't think Eric is the right person." She said the words with a smile, though they really only made her sad. Life would be so much easier if all choices came with clearly marked Right and Wrong signs on them.

She saw Eric briefly that afternoon, when he and Maddie delivered an elderly man who turned out to be suffering from altitude sickness. Neither paramedic wore a costume. "We didn't want to send some poor patient into cardiac arrest by showing up as zombies or anything," Eric explained.

"I worried about that at the hospital, but so far the patients seem to enjoy the costumes," she said. "And a group of children from a local day care center came through this afternoon, trick-or-treating. They were very cute. Lots of little princesses and witches and superheroes."

"You're cute," he said. "I never liked cats much, but you could change my mind."

"You'd better get back to work," she chided, fighting down a blush.

"Don't forget the party tomorrow," he said. "You won't need a costume for that. Just come as yourself."

"Should I bring something? Food to share?"

He laughed. "My mom and sisters and aunts have made enough food to feed half of Gunnison. Don't worry."

She went to bed that evening and dreamed of sweet little princesses being chased by superheroes carrying sugar skulls.

PROMPTLY AT NOON the next day, Eric arrived to drive Alina to his house. He'd told his mother he was bringing "a friend" but hadn't elaborated. He didn't want his parents to make too much of the fact that he'd invited Alina to their home again. Though they'd welcomed her as a guest before, they might feel differently if they thought Eric was getting serious about someone from such a different background. They had very traditional ideas and believed people could be happy in marriage if they shared the same culture.

If they had any objections, he didn't want to hear them before they'd even had a chance to really know Alina. Once they'd spent more time with her, he was sure they'd see what a great person she was.

"Tell me more about this day of the dead," she said as he drove toward his neighborhood. "Do you do anything besides have a party?"

"My mom attended Mass this morning, then all of us went to the cemetery to decorate the graves of our relatives," he said. "Some people like to leave favorite foods or candy or even liquor on the graves. And there are always flowers, usually marigolds."

"Why marigolds?" she asked.

"I think the dead are supposed to like them." He cut his eyes at her. "I'm not saying I believe all this, but it's tradition. Something my grandparents brought with them from Mexico."

"I understand," she said. "We have traditions like that in my country, too."

"Tell me one of your traditions."

"Let's see. At weddings, guests are given rosemary to pin on their clothes, like a little corsage."

"Why rosemary?"

"I don't know. It's just something we do. Whenever I smell rosemary, I think of my sisters' weddings."

He laughed. "Whenever I smell rosemary, I think of roast chicken."

"I guess all traditions can look silly to outsiders," she conceded. "But it's good to have customs and foods and ways of doing things that can link a group of people together. Life can change, but those little things that are always the same provide continuity through generations."

"I've never thought about it that way," Eric said.

"I might not have, either, except that my father studies traditions and customs and writes about them as part of his job at the university. I guess I've picked up a few ideas from him over the years."

"I'm sure my family could give him plenty to write about," Eric said. "We have a tradition for everything— sometimes even I have trouble keeping up."

"But you do," Alina said.

"Yeah, most of the time I do. Even when I don't understand why we do it, it feels good to be part of something so familiar." His family's traditions were part of who he was; forgetting them would be like losing part of himself.

"Maybe it's easier to look to the future when you feel anchored in the past," she said.

"Maybe so." Or maybe he couldn't see a future without certain traditions and customs as part of it.

The driveway at Eric's parents' house was crowded with cars, but he managed to find a parking spot at the curb. As he and Alina crossed the lawn to the front door, he was surprised to see Marissa walking toward them.

"Marissa, what are you doing here?" Alina asked.

"Mrs. Sepulveda invited me," she said. "Wasn't that sweet?"

"Yeah, sweet," Eric said. Was his mother simply being nice or was she up to something?

They found Marty in the house with Eric's brothers,

John, Gilberto, Jaime and Bart. "Did Mrs. Sepulveda invite you to the party, too?" Marissa asked.

"Eric's parents have practically adopted me," Marty said. "I'm over here so much."

"You just hang around for the food," Eric said.

"Hey, you know me—I never turn down a free meal."

"Blessings to you all." Eric's mother entered, bearing a tray of anise seed cookies and pieces of candied pumpkin. She stopped in front of Alina and Marissa. "It's good to see you girls again," she said. "Marty, show Alina where she can leave her purse. Marissa, you and Eric come help me in the kitchen."

Eric started to protest, but Alina was already following Marty out of the room, so he trailed after his mother and Marissa.

The two women conversed in Spanish—something about the dress Marissa wore, which looked pretty much like the dresses other women wore as far as Eric could tell. "You two put ice in glasses and carry them into the dining room," his mother instructed.

After they'd filled the glasses, Eric helped Marissa grate cheese and chop lettuce. "I should check on Alina," he said. "I don't want to be rude to a guest."

"Marty will take care of her," his mother said, her expression revealing nothing.

Once, passing from the kitchen to the dining room, Eric caught sight of Alina and Marty. They stood in a side room, studying the altar that had been set up to honor the family dead. The small table was crowded with photographs of deceased relatives, flowers, candy skulls and the fancily dressed skeletons known as *catrinas*.

Did Alina think such a celebration was odd, or did she have customs in her country that were just as strange to outsiders? And did she think it strange that Eric had invited her to this party and then abandoned her? He'd have to find a way to apologize later—and to outsmart his mother's manipulations.

AT DINNER, Alina found herself seated between Marty and one of Eric's young cousins. Eric sat with Marissa at the other end of the table. Alina caught his eye and smiled, and he gave her an apologetic look. She nodded at his mother, a sign that she understood. Eric's mother clearly thought Marissa was a more suitable partner for her son, and was doing her best to throw them together.

At the same time, she was making sure that Alina and Marty had plenty of opportunity to get to know each other better. Marty had explained to her that on the Day of the Dead, those who had gone on before were thought to be close by their loved ones, celebrating with them, as it were. Hence the offerings of favorite food and drinks and fresh flowers.

Was Alina's grandmother close to her today? Was she conspiring with Mrs. Sepulveda to push Alina toward Marty, or was she only standing by and nodding in approval?

Alina did her best to ignore the queasy feeling that came over her whenever she glanced down the table and saw Marissa and Eric laughing together. She knew her friend had no interest in Eric; that very week Marissa had confided she was dating a new intern at the hospital and she liked him very much.

Alina forced herself to focus on Marty. "How long have you known Eric?" she asked.

"Since I came to Gunnison about a year and a half ago," Marty said. "When I joined the EMS, he and I hit it off."

"And you've spent a lot of time with his family?"

"The first time he invited me over, I raved about the food so much, Mrs. Sepulveda must have thought I was starving. My parents are out of the country right now, on a missionary trip to South America, so she takes pity on me and invites me for holidays and family dinners." He lowered his voice. "I suspect she thinks that since I'm a seminary student, I'll be a good influence on Eric."

"Oh? Does he need a good influence?"

"No. He's a great guy. Not wild like some guys our age. But all his brothers and sisters married when they were younger than Eric is now, so I think she's worried he'll never settle down."

"Twenty-six isn't so old to still be single." This was something she told herself often.

"No. But you know how it is with family."

She nodded. When you were close to your family, you wanted to please them, yet you also struggled to be your own person.

After supper, each person received a little sugar skull decorated with sugar flowers, and little round sweet buns called *pan de muerto*. Alina bit into hers cautiously. "Very good," she said, nodding.

"I think it would be better with jam," Marty confided. "But it's not bad."

"Let me help with the dishes," Marissa said.

"No, no. You stay and visit with Eric," Mrs. Sepulveda said.

"I could help," Alina offered, though the thought of being stuck in the kitchen alone with Mrs. Sepulveda made her knees tremble.

"I'll help with the dishes." Sofia made a shooing motion. "You two are our guests. Relax and visit." She followed her mother into the kitchen.

"Yeah, we'll get out the family photos and show you pictures of Eric when he was a kid," John said.

"I'm pretty sure there's one somewhere of him in a school play where he played a frog," Bart added.

"Were you really a frog, Uncle Eric?" Emma asked.

"Warts and all," Bart said.

Eric glared at his brother, his eyes sending the message that Bart would pay later for that remark. "Alina and I really need to be going," he said. "We both have to be at work early tomorrow."

Alina didn't have to be at work any earlier than usual, but she didn't object when Eric ushered her out the door. "I hope you don't mind we ducked out early," he said when they were settled in his truck. "I wanted some time alone with you without my family putting in their two cents."

"You have a very nice family," she said.

"Yeah, but they make it hard to make a good impression on a girl sometimes."

The fact that he wanted to impress her pleased her, but she maintained a solemn expression. "I'm sure you were a very cute frog," she said.

He laughed. "I don't really have to be at work that early

tomorrow," he said. "Why don't we go somewhere where we can talk? We could get coffee or have a drink…"

A coffee shop or bar would allow them privacy to talk, but they wouldn't really be alone. "We could go to my place," she said. "I could make coffee."

His eyes met hers, alert, questioning. "If you're sure that's not too much trouble."

"Of course not." Though being alone with him might very well lead to trouble…the kind of trouble *Baka* Fania most certainly would not approve of.

Chapter Seven

Eric had learned a lot about Alina in the short time they'd been together. He'd seen how compassionate and encouraging she was with her patients, and how fond they were of her in return. He knew how when she thought something was funny she abandoned herself to mirth, her whole being suffused with laughter. Despite her excellent English, her struggles to interpret slang and idioms charmed him. She liked to wear blue and purple. She loved sweets, but stayed away from very spicy foods. She used a shampoo that made her hair smell like vanilla.

He'd cataloged all these details in his mind, little tidbits that added up to the whole. He wouldn't have hesitated to say he knew her well, but seeing her apartment added a new dimension to the woman. The intimacy of being invited into her private space made him more aware than ever of his feelings for her. Alina wasn't just a pretty woman to him—she was someone he was beginning to care about a great deal.

"It isn't much," she said, leading him into the living

room. "The furniture isn't mine, but I've tried to decorate with a few things, to make it more homey."

A large flag with three bars of red, white and blue and a red-and-white checked shield in the center hung over the sofa. "The Croatian flag," she said when she saw it had caught his attention. "My father sent it to me. He is a great patriot."

A bright scarf draped over the back of a chair lent more color to the room, and an arrangement of dried branches and grasses in a large urn on the coffee table looked like something out of one of those decorating magazines his sisters liked to read. "Did you do this?" he asked, touching the tip of one branch.

She shrugged. "It is just things I gathered from the side of the road. I thought they were pretty."

"They are. It looks great." He turned to her. "You're great." It seemed a cliché to say he'd never met anyone like her, but it was true. The women he'd dated before had been all of a type: pretty, athletic, intelligent and fun. Alina was all of those, but while the other women in his life had been easy to read, from a background much like his own, Alina had an aura of mystery. Not as outspoken as most of the American women he knew, she had secrets he couldn't wait to discover.

"Would you like something to drink?" she asked. "I have tea and coffee, and maybe some orange juice…"

"Nothing to drink. Why don't we sit down and talk." He sat on the sofa and patted the cushion beside him.

She hesitated, then settled next to him. "What do you want to talk about?"

"Tell me about growing up in Croatia. What was it like? What's your family like?"

"I didn't have a very big family like yours," she said. "But in a way the whole village was my family. We did things together, celebrated holidays with local festivals and big meals and dancing." Her expression softened, and her smile grew wistful. "My two sisters and I would dress in old-fashioned costumes and dance with my mother and aunts and other women from the village. And my grandmother taught us to make all the traditional dishes—*palacinka,* which is a dessert made with sweet cakes and jam and chocolate, and *sarma,* made with cabbage and meat and spices, and *pasticada,* a kind of marinated beef."

"Maybe you could make those for me some time," he said.

She laughed. "Maybe I will, though it's been a long time since I did much cooking. Even my mother prefers to buy things ready-made these days. My grandmother was really the cook in the family and after she passed we didn't eat as well."

"I remember you said your grandmother lived with you. Was that the whole time you were growing up?"

Alina nodded. "All my life. My grandfather died right before I was born. *Baka* Fania always said I was sent from heaven to comfort her. She always said I was her favorite, though I suspect she told my sisters and cousins the same things. I have a picture." She jumped up and retrieved her purse from the kitchen counter. She returned with an open wallet. "The tiny lady in the long skirt is my grandmother. The woman with the dark hair is my mother and in the middle is me. That was taken a couple of years ago, shortly before *Baka* Fania died."

Eric studied the picture of the three women. Alina looked much as she did now, though her hair was a little shorter in the photograph and her clothes were not as stylish. Her mother's head was turned slightly, so that she smiled at the other two instead of the camera.

Alina's grandmother stared out of the photograph with a fierce gaze, her mouth set in a hard line. "She looks like someone I wouldn't want to cross," he said, returning the photo to her.

"You wouldn't," Alina agreed. She smiled at the picture. "*Baka* Fania was half gypsy and was said to have the power to predict the future—and to put curses on people."

"Seriously? Curses? Did she ever do it?"

"Not that I know of. But she always told people she could, and that was enough to make everyone a little bit afraid of her. No shopkeepers ever tried to cheat her, and people went out of their way to be nice to her."

Sadness filled her eyes. Eric hesitated, then put his arm around her. "You miss her, don't you?"

She swallowed hard. "I do. My parents are good people and I love them, but *Baka* Fania was special. My parents had to work, but she had time to teach me things or to sit and talk. I learned so much from her."

He rubbed her shoulder, wanting to comfort her. "She sounds like a wonderful woman. I wish I could have met her."

"She would have liked you, I think, but she might have pretended not to," Alina said.

"Why is that?"

"Because she always said never to trust a dark-eyed, handsome man." She looked at him, eyes sparkling once more. "I've seen pictures of my grandfather as a young man, and *he* was very handsome with dark eyes. I think you would remind her of him."

"I guess *Baka* means grandmother in Croatian?"

"Yes."

"Teach me some other Croatian words."

"All right." She looked around them, then picked up a book from the coffee table. *"Knjiga."*

"What's this?" He touched her arm.

"Ruka."

"And this?" He stroked her hair.

"Kosa."

"And this?" He put a finger to her lips.

"Usta." Her voice grew breathy.

"How do you say *kiss* in Croatian?"

"Lagan dodir biljarskih kugala."

"Lagan dodir biljarskih kugala," he repeated, then covered her lips with his own.

The kiss was tender yet urgent. She slipped her arms around his neck and arched against him, abandoning herself to the kiss the way she surrendered to laughter, her whole being involved. Eric gathered her to him and deepened the kiss, aware of how little time he might have left with her. He wanted to savor every moment, take advantage of every opportunity to taste and feel and *be* with her.

They were both breathless when they finally pulled

away from each other. She stared at him, wide-eyed. "Do you believe in fate?" she asked.

He blinked. "Do you mean…like, two people meant to be together?"

She nodded, her gaze searching his, as if his answer was desperately important.

"I don't know," he said. "Do you?"

She wet her lips, and looked away. "*Baka* Fania did. She believed the plan for our lives was laid out at birth and trying to change it only got a person into trouble."

"I don't believe in that kind of fate," he said. "I believe we each chart our own course in life, though tradition and how we're raised may influence the choices we make." He tightened his grip on her. "I can't predict the future, but I know what I want right now."

Her eyes met his again, dark and luminous. "I know what I want also," she said. She brushed the hair back from his forehead. "I want you to stay here with me tonight."

THE VOICE IN ALINA'S HEAD that told her what she was doing was wrong was drowned out by her belief that this was the most right thing she'd ever done. She didn't have much more time with Eric, and whatever her future held—wherever fate or her own choices led her—she wanted to have the memory of this time with him.

Someone had once told her that it wasn't what a person did in life they would regret most, but what they didn't do. She had never fully understood that sentiment until now. She knew if she didn't act on her feelings for Eric, if she didn't spend at least this one night with him, she would regret it forever.

"My bedroom is back here," she said. She took his hand and led him down the hall, feeling shy but excited, too, like a child at Christmas or on her birthday. She knew something wonderful was in store for her.

For a man who radiated such strength and energy, he was touchingly gentle with her, helping her undress, kissing her shoulder as she slipped off her blouse, steadying her as she stepped out of her pants.

"You're beautiful," he said, when she stood before him in a pink bra and panties.

"No fair," she said. "You shouldn't be the only one getting to look." She fumbled impatiently with the top button of his shirt.

Together they undid the remaining buttons and stripped off the garment. His jeans soon followed. Alina smoothed her hand across his abdomen, a flutter of arousal running through her own stomach as she admired him. He was absolutely perfect.

"Now *I'm* getting self-conscious with you staring at me that way," he said.

"What way?" She looked up at him through the curtain of her lowered lashes, pretending innocence.

"Sort of…greedily."

"And this is a bad thing?"

"Not really." He pulled her close. "It's good to think you want me as much as I want you." He kissed her long and hard until she felt light-headed, as if she was floating.

He led her to the bed, and they lay side by side, exchanging shy smiles, moving on to tender touching which became more passionate as impatience overcame the novelty of this first encounter. Soon they were completely naked, bare skin to bare skin. Alina felt more beautiful and sexy and *happy* than she had in a long time.

Then, in the middle of a passionate kiss, Eric went still. "What is it?" she asked as he pulled away from her.

"Um, we should probably do something about protection."

"I have some." Reaching across him, she opened the drawer of the bedside table and pulled out a string of condoms.

She laughed at the expression on his face when she presented him with this prize. He didn't hide his emotions well. Clearly he wondered why she was so well prepared. "I work in a hospital," she said. "We give these away for free. And my mother and sisters all gave me condoms to pack for the trip here. They obviously thought America was the land of nonstop orgies."

He looked relieved. "I guess if you watch some American television shows, you could think that."

She did her best to look solemn. "I was very disappointed. I haven't been invited to a single orgy in all the months I've been here. Not even a little one."

"I'll have to see if I can make up for that."

He opened the condom and she watched, transfixed, as he rolled it on. Then she rolled into his arms again. "I don't need an orgy," she said. "One man is plenty for me—if he's the right man."

"I'll do my best to be the right man."

All doubts about the choice she'd made that night, and all thoughts of any other man, blond or not, fled from her mind as he moved over her and into her. She wanted to shout with delight, but settled for grinning up at him, tracing her hands along his muscular body, reveling in his strength and beauty.

But the most beautiful thing about him was the way he looked at her, and the tenderness and passion with which he touched her. They moved together in perfect rhythm, the sensations building until she cried out with pleasure, and he followed soon after, his strong arms around her, lifting her and holding her. In those moments she had never felt more cherished.

They lay together afterward, saying little, touching often. She drifted to sleep with a smile on her face, her hand in his, determined to hold on to these feelings and this man until she had no choice but to let him go.

ERIC WOKE THE NEXT MORNING to the ringing of a cell phone. *His* cell phone, but it wasn't in its usual spot on the nightstand. The nightstand wasn't there, either. When he finally burrowed out from under the covers and opened his eyes, nothing looked familiar.

"What is that noise?"

Alina's sleepy voice woke Eric fully. The events of the night before came rushing back and he smiled and rolled toward her. "Good morning, beautiful," he said.

"Is that your phone?" She twisted her head around to look at the heap of clothing on the floor. From somewhere in the pile, strains of salsa music floated up.

"Whoever it is, they'll leave a message," he said, and tried to pull her close again.

"You should answer it," she said. "What if it's an emergency?"

The phone fell silent. Relieved, he slid farther down

under the covers and tried to drag her with him. But his head had scarcely touched the pillow again when the phone jangled once more.

"You'd better get it," Alina said.

Grudgingly, he rolled to the edge of the bed and threw back the covers. He was halfway to the pile of clothes when she cried out. "Wait. Don't answer it!"

He bent and retrieved the phone, which vibrated in his hands. "Why not?"

"What if it's your parents calling to find out why you didn't come home last night?"

"Alina, I'm twenty-six. My parents don't check up on me."

"Mine would."

He glanced at the phone's display. "It's okay. It's just Marty."

Before she could object further, he flipped open the phone. "Hey, Marty."

"Sorry to bother you, but I need to see if you can trade shifts with me tonight. I've got a big test tomorrow I need to cram for."

"Sure. No problemo."

"I stopped by your house, but your mom said you didn't come home last night."

"No, I didn't." Eric grinned, letting the tension build.

Alina sat up in bed and gathered the sheets around her. Her hair fell in tousled waves around her shoulders and her expression was soft and sleepy. He fought the urge to hang up on his friend and immediately crawl back into bed with her.

"So where are you?"

"With a friend."

Alina's eyebrows rose and she shaped her lips into a pout.

"Are you with Alina?" Marty laughed. "I should have guessed. Okay, I won't ask any more."

"Good. Because I won't answer any more. Talk to you later."

He hung up without waiting for a response, and leaped back into bed, bouncing onto the mattress. "Are you going to tell him you were with me?" she asked.

"He already guessed." He kissed her cheek. "He knows how much I like you, and we did leave my parents' house together last night."

"Then your parents have probably guessed, too." She nibbled her lower lip. "What will they say?"

"They won't say anything. Believe me, my parents don't talk about my sex life. They'd like to pretend I don't have one."

"Your mother doesn't approve of me."

"She likes you," he protested. "How could she not?"

"She thinks Marissa is a better match. She keeps trying to throw the two of you together. And she thinks I belong with Marty."

"But I don't want to be with Marissa. I want to be with you." He didn't want to have this conversation with her. His mother was only interested in marrying him off to someone she considered suitable. Marriage wasn't something he wanted to think about right now—and probably not for a long time yet.

He tried to pull Alina close, but she gently shoved him away. "I have to get ready for work," she said.

He glanced at the clock. "We have time for a quickie."

"No!" She slapped him away, laughing.

He flopped back on the bed and enjoyed watching her rush around the room, gathering up clothes before she disappeared into the bathroom. He heard the shower running and debated joining her, but decided he'd better not push his luck. He sat up and was reaching for his jeans when his phone rang again.

This time it was his sister Sofia. "Bart says you never came home last night," she said. "He thinks you spent the night with Alina. Is that true?"

"What business is it of yours?" He cradled the phone against his shoulder and pulled on his jeans.

"None of my business, but I'm asking anyway. Did you spend the night with her?"

"I'll never tell."

"Such a gentleman." She made a tsking sound. "I'm guessing you did. I saw the way you were looking at her yesterday at Mom and Dad's."

"I wasn't looking at her any particular way." Give him credit for being cool enough not to moon over a woman in public—especially not in front of his parents.

"You couldn't keep your eyes off her. It was so obvious."

"So I like her. What's wrong with that?"

"Nothing. She's a very nice girl. But isn't she leaving in a couple of months to go back to Croatia?"

"Well, yeah."

"You want more than a pretty face for a wife. You want someone you can build a life with."

"Who said anything about a wife?" His voice rose.

He glanced toward the bathroom door. The shower was still running, so Alina probably hadn't heard. He lowered his voice. "I have four years of medical school and several years after that of training before I can even think about getting married."

"I hear Mama and *Abuelita* have different plans."

"Come on, Sofia. This is the twenty-first century. My mother can't choose a woman for me and make me marry her."

"Tell that to Guillermo. When those two decide you're going to get married, you're going to marry someone, if only to stop them from making your life miserable."

"That's ridiculous. Besides, the only reason they want me to marry now is because they think it will make me stay home and forget the idea of becoming a doctor."

"You're the one who's been saying you can't marry and go to school at the same time, so you could say you gave them the idea to play matchmakers."

"The folks are worried I don't know what I'm getting into here, that I'll drown in debt or work myself to death. But I'm not naive—I know what I want to do is hard. It's going to take everything I've got not to fail. So, yes, I won't let a relationship with a woman—whether it's one Mom chooses or one I find on my own—sidetrack me from my dream."

"I know you won't fail," Sofia said. "And I'll do anything I can to help you."

"Then run interference," he pleaded. "Tell Mom I'm hopeless. Tell her no woman would have me."

"Coward," Sofia said. "But I'm not so sure they're wrong about the marriage idea."

"I told you—"

She hastened to silence his protests. "Not because I think you need to be tied down here at home," she said. "But haven't you heard a burden is easier to carry with a partner? A wife could help out financially, too. And you don't want to be an old man with little kids running around."

"I'm only two years younger than you."

"And I've been married ten years. Listen to your mother. Marriage would be good for you. Stop wasting your time with unattainable women like Alina and find someone from *this* country. I know a few girls I could introduce you to."

"No, thanks. When I'm ready I can find my own. Right now, I'm enjoying Alina. At least until she leaves in January."

"So you *did* spend the night with her. I knew it!" Laughing, she hung up on him.

Eric stared at the phone, debating calling her back and telling her to stay out of his business. But Sofia never listened to anyone, least of all her younger brother.

The bathroom door opened, and Alina emerged, damp hair curling around her face, the aroma of her vanilla shampoo trailing after her. "I wish I didn't have to leave," she said.

"Me, too." He kissed her cheek, then her lips. "I have to work tonight, but I'll call you. And we'll see each other again soon." With so little time left, he didn't want to waste a moment. Maybe he couldn't love Alina forever, but he could love her right now, and that was all that mattered.

Chapter Eight

Alina floated in a fog of happiness much of the next two weeks. Though work schedules and other commitments kept her and Eric from seeing each other as much as they might have liked, they ran into each other at the hospital frequently, and spent two more magical nights together.

Only the arrival of Alina's parents brought her back down to earth. While she was overjoyed to see them again, their presence reminded her of her impending return to Croatia and of *Baka* Fania's prediction that a blond man—not a dark-haired one with laughing brown eyes—held the key to her future happiness.

"Alina, darling!" Her mother enveloped her in a mighty hug as soon as she spotted her daughter waiting at the baggage claim in the little Gunnison airport. She kissed Alina soundly on both cheeks, then stepped back to admire her. Dressed in the brown cloth coat she'd worn for years, a yards-long green woolen scarf wrapped around and around her neck, Jelena Allinova smelled of the menthol salve she believe warded off all the germs one was certain to encounter in traveling. Her face was heavily powdered and her coral lip-stick had faded, but to Alina she appeared not to have changed a bit in the nine months they'd been parted.

Her father, a tall man who perpetually hunched over as if avoiding too-low doorways and ceilings, waved at her from the baggage carousel, where he scrutinized each suitcase that passed.

"Let me look at you!" Her mother held her at arm's length. "Your hair is longer," she said. "And are those new clothes? You look so American!"

"Mom, these are the same jeans I had in Croatia, but the shirt is new, yes." The Croatian words rolled off her tongue. It felt good to speak her native language again.

While her father snagged their luggage, Alina's mother poured out all the details of the trip. "You should have seen the crowds at the airport in Dubrovnik! Then, in Denver, we had to walk miles to our gate. I thought we would never get there. On the plane they wouldn't give us anything to eat—not even a package of peanuts. We had to pay for a bag of pretzels. They even wanted to charge us for blankets!"

"I'm glad you're here now," Alina said. "We'll eat and rest and you'll feel much better tomorrow."

When all four of her parents' suitcases had been piled onto a luggage cart, Alina led the way to the parking lot to the Subaru wagon a coworker had sold her her first week at her new job. "They must pay you well," her father observed, patting the top of the little blue car, "to afford a nice car like this."

"It wasn't that expensive." She settled into the driver's

seat and buckled her seat belt. "Do you want to look around first, or go straight to my apartment?" she asked.

"We need to go to your apartment," her mother said. "I have things to unpack."

Alina suspected this meant perishable cheeses or sausage, but decided not to ask.

At her apartment, she helped haul the suitcases up the stairs. "Mom, what did you pack in here?" she asked. "These weigh a ton."

"Just clothes and some things I thought you might need. A few jars of *ajvar,* some cans of figs and capers."

"Mom, they have grocery stores in Gunnison. Big ones, with everything I could need."

"But they don't have real Croatian food like this." Her mother arranged a pyramid of colorful cans on the countertop and beamed. "And I brought you this, too." She offered a small plastic bag.

"What is it?" To Alina, the bag looked empty.

"It's the wheat seeds for planting on St. Lucy's Day."

Now Alina noticed the small grains bunched in one corner of the bag. "Aww, Mom." She hugged her mother close. "That was so sweet of you to remember." In Croatia, on December 13, which was St. Lucy's Day, families planted wheat in shallow dishes of water. It sprouted and grew tall until Christmas Eve, when the stalks were tied with red, white and blue ribbon and used as a centerpiece. As the youngest girl, Alina had always been given the honor of "planting" the wheat in a shallow dish.

"I know they have wheat in the United States," her mother said. "But this is Croatian wheat for the Croatian holiday celebration."

"Thank you, Mom. I'll keep it safe until St. Lucy's Day." She tucked the bag of seeds in a kitchen drawer, next to boxes of tea and packets of sugar. She was glad for the opportunity to turn away for a moment and gather herself. The wheat reminded her that she wouldn't be spending the holidays at home this year, but by herself in a place where she didn't really know the traditions and customs.

"This is a very nice apartment." Her father's voice pulled her back from bleak thoughts of the future. She turned to find him rubbing the material of the kitchen curtains between his thumb and forefinger. "It must be expensive."

"It's not, Dad. Really."

Her mother bustled about the kitchen, opening cabinets and drawers. "Mom, what are you doing?" Alina asked.

"I thought I'd make coffee. And maybe a little snack. I'm sure your father's hungry."

"I'm not hungry," her father said.

"Of course you are. You've hardly eaten all day. Alina, where do you keep your coffee?"

"I'll make the coffee," Alina said. "And some sandwiches. You sit and rest. You're my guests. I should wait on you."

"I'm your *mother*," she protested, but she sat at the little table where Alina ate most of her meals. "Do you have any ham?" she asked. "Your father loves ham sandwiches."

"I'll make you both ham sandwiches."

While Alina prepared lunch, her father inspected

every item in the living room, from the furniture to the pictures on the walls and books on her shelves. Her mother continued her complaints about the long flight, crowded airports and unhelpful people she'd encountered on the trip from Croatia.

Alina's father had disappeared down the hall by the time she set the sandwiches and coffee on the table. Alina retrieved him before he could inspect the bathroom cabinets and her closet, though, knowing her dad, such scrutiny was inevitable.

"Have you dated many American men?" her mother asked when they were all seated around the table.

"Not many." Alina concentrated on her sandwich, avoiding her mother's eyes. "I've been very busy with work."

"You don't work all the time." Her mother smoothed her own hair, which was carefully dyed the same dark brown she'd been born with. "Croatian women are known for their beauty, so I know men must have asked you out."

"How could they not?" her father said.

"There are a lot of beautiful women in America, too," Alina said.

"Are you seeing anyone right now?" her mother asked.

"Not really," she lied. She wasn't ready to tell her parents about Eric. What was the point? After she moved home, she probably wouldn't see him again. The thought caused a pain around her heart. She gulped hot coffee as if that could drown the pain. "I thought tomorrow we could drive up to Crested Butte," she said. "There's a ski resort there and a friend of mine got lift tickets." Eric had offered the tickets when he'd heard her father liked to ski.

"Skiing?" Her father's face lit up. "I hear Colorado has excellent snow," he said. "Champagne powder."

"I think that's Steamboat, Colorado, Dad, but the snow in Crested Butte is very good," she said. "You'll like it." And getting out on the slopes would be a good way to avoid an entire day of questions about her personal life.

THE NEXT MORNING, Alina woke to the smell of fresh coffee and frying sausages. She shuffled into the kitchen and found her mom, a towel wrapped around her waist in lieu of an apron, standing at the stove. Her father, in ski pants and a Nordic sweater, sat at the table, reading an academic text on Slavic social history. "Mom, what are you doing?" Alina asked.

"What does it look like I'm doing? I'm making breakfast." She adjusted the towel. "I can tell you haven't eaten a proper meal since you left home. You don't even own an apron and these pots and pans look as if you've hardly used them."

"There's no need for me to cook big meals for one person," Alina said.

"When you marry, you'll need to cook for your husband, and then your family. You should stay in practice." She cracked an egg on the side of a bowl and added salt. "Sit, and I'll cook you a nice breakfast."

Alina sat. She'd grown used to fending for herself these past months, but maybe her mother needed to look after her daughter for a while. It wouldn't hurt Alina to humor her.

After breakfast, Alina hurried her parents into her car

for the drive to Crested Butte. Her father sat in the passenger seat, his camera pointed out the window, documenting every mile with photos of the snowy expanse of prairie relieved only by the occasional hay barn or cluster of cattle, or a line of deer pawing at the deepening snow.

At the entrance to Crested Butte, he made her stop so he could take pictures of the dragon in front of the Center for the Arts. Then he insisted they detour down Elk Avenue, "So that I can see a typical American small town."

"Dad, there's nothing typical about Crested Butte," she said, but drove slowly past the lines of colorful Victorian storefronts on the town's main street while his camera clicked away.

"I want coffee," her mother said as they neared Trish's coffee shop.

"We just had breakfast," Alina protested. At this rate, they wouldn't reach the ski slopes until noon.

"And now I want coffee. And maybe a pastry."

Stifling a sigh, Alina found a parking space a block up from the coffee shop, and the three of them walked back to the narrow yellow building. A string of sleigh bells attached to the back of the door announced their arrival.

"Alina!" Zephyr, clad in bright green snowboarding pants, a gray fleece and a green-and-white stocking cap, the tip of which hung past his knees, greeted them at the door. *"Hasta la vista. Que paso?"*

"Zephyr, Alina is from Croatia, not Mexico." Trish spoke from behind the counter. She shook her head at her boyfriend and sent Alina an apologetic look.

"Yeah, but Spanish is the only foreign language I

know." Zephyr grinned good-naturedly. He turned to Alina's mother and father. "And who is this?"

"This is my mother and father," Alina said. "They're visiting from Croatia."

"Awesome. Always great to meet parental units." He stuck out his hand. "My name's Zephyr. Alina's probably told you about me."

"Hello." Alina's mom shook Zephyr's hand and gave her daughter a questioning look. "Alina has told us about so many people…"

"Zephyr's only famous in his own mind," Trish said. "What can I get you folks?"

"Coffee." Mrs. Allinova approached the front counter. "And a pastry." She pointed to a frosted bun.

"A bear claw," Trish said, and slid one of the delicacies onto a plate.

Alina's mother laughed. "What a funny name."

"It's not really a bear's claw," Zephyr said. He came to stand beside her. "It just sort of looks like one. Well, not the claw, really, but the whole bear's *paw.* But see, the little almonds on the ends sort of look like the claws."

Alina's mother stared at him, wide-eyed, and nodded.

"Coffee for me," Alina's father said. "Nothing to eat." He sat at one of the little tables.

Zephyr plopped into the chair beside him. "You folks headed to the slopes?" he asked.

"We are going skiing, yes." Alina's father frowned at the strange young man with the wild dreadlocks sticking out from beneath the stocking cap. Alina wondered if he was thinking of writing a paper on unusual Americans. Zephyr could be his first subject.

"Awesome pow up there today," Zephyr said. "Stellar for November. There are some serious stashes and sick runs."

Alina looked at Trish.

"He means there's a lot of fresh snow," Trish translated. "The skiing should be good." She delivered two cups of coffee and the pastry, then rang up the sale and handed Alina her change.

"Hey, it was great meeting you." Zephyr stood and shook hands with Mr. and Mrs. Allinova. "I gotta go, but I'm sure I'll see you around."

Alina's mom waited until the sound of the ringing sleigh bells had died in Zephyr's wake. "Please tell me that is not your boyfriend," she said.

"No," Alina said. "He lives with Trish."

"That's me," Trish said. "I'm the lucky gal."

"Oh, I am sure he is a fine young man," Mrs. Allinova said.

"He's just a friend, Mom. Really."

Mrs. Allinova nodded and took a bite of bear claw. "It's very good." She nodded approvingly. "And the almonds do look like little claws."

Coffee and pastry consumed, they thanked Trish and hit the road again, finally arriving in the ski area parking lot. "Such a big place," her father enthused as they headed for the rental shop.

"Look at all the stores." Her mother craned her neck to study a display of ski gear in a window. "We must visit them later."

"First, we ski." Her father took his wife's arm and hurried her to the rental shop.

Thanks to their late arrival, they didn't have to wait to rent equipment and in a short time they were fitted with skis, boots and poles. As they emerged from the shop and turned toward the lifts, Alina's heart skipped a beat at the sight of a familiar dark-haired figure striding toward them.

The red patroller's jacket emphasized Eric's broad shoulders and narrow waist and set off the brown of his eyes. When he smiled, Alina felt her insides quiver. Fearful of giving away too much of her feelings, she turned to her parents. "Mom, Dad, this is the friend who gave us the lift tickets—Eric Sepulveda. He's with Crested Butte Ski Patrol."

"Hello!" Her mother beamed, looking almost girlish. "It is so nice to meet you, Alina's handsome friend."

"Thank you for the lift tickets," her father said solemnly, and looked longingly toward the lift.

"I'm happy to meet you both," Eric said. "Would you like me to show you around the slopes?"

"That would be great," Alina said. Any excuse to spend a little more time with him, even in the company of her parents.

With Eric as their escort, they moved to the front of the lift line. On the way up the mountain, he chatted about the history of the resort and some of the runs. Alina listened in silence, content to bask in the soft cadence of his speech and the solid warmth of him in the chair beside her.

By their third run, it was clear her parents were impressed. Eric listened patiently to her father's long scientific discussion about the moisture content of the snow, and complimented her mother on her skiing form, then winked at Alina over the head of her beaming parent. Alina fell a little bit more in love with him in that moment, the steepness of the ski runs presenting no challenge at all compared to the recklessness of admitting her feelings for him.

They took a break for lunch in a small restaurant at the base of the slopes. "Most of these buildings are new," Eric explained as he led them to a round table at the back of the room. "They were constructed as part of a number of improvements to the resort."

"Hey, Eric! Alina!" A burly figure clad all in black strode toward them. Marty stopped at their table and pulled off his helmet, revealing a wild tangle of blond hair. "Hello," he nodded to Alina's parents.

"Marty, these are my parents," Alina said. "Mom, Dad, this is Marty Padgett."

Alina's mother studied the man before her, her gaze coming to rest on his hair. "It is a pleasure to meet you, Mr. Padgett," she said. "Will you join us for luncheon?"

"Thank you, but I promised some friends from school I'd meet them over at the Paradise Warming Hut," he said. "I just wanted to say hi. Welcome to Colorado."

"I need to check in with patrol," Eric said. "If you'll excuse me for a minute." He walked with Marty toward the door.

"Mr. Padgett seems very nice," Alina's mother said as soon as the men had left the building. "He is in school?"

"He's studying to be a minister."

Mrs. Allinova's smile broadened. "A very respectable young man. Have you dated him?"

Alina almost choked on her hamburger. "No!"

"Why not? Is he married?"

"No, he's not married." She glanced over her shoulder to make sure no one she knew was close enough to hear, then lowered her voice anyway. "He hasn't asked me out." Not to mention she wasn't interested in Marty.

"Then you should ask him."

"Mom! I can't do that."

"Why not? This is the twenty-first century. This is America, home of liberated women. You can ask a man out."

"I could, but I don't want to."

"Are you forgetting what your grandmother told you? He could be the one."

"I don't know, Mom. If he was the one, wouldn't he ask me out? And if he was the one, wouldn't I feel at least *some* attraction to him?"

"Maybe not. Some men need a little coaxing." She looked at Alina's father, who was engrossed in a study of the trail map.

"Mom, are you telling me you pursued Dad?"

"I nudged him a little. He was so consumed by his studies, he didn't notice me until I made sure he couldn't ignore me."

This revelation fascinated Alina. She'd never thought much about her parents' courtship. They'd grown up in the same town, and her mother had told her they'd been introduced by a mutual friend. Alina had assumed they'd fallen in love at first sight.

"Mom, what did you do?"

"I showed up at his apartment late one winter night. There was a storm and I told him my car had broken down near his apartment."

Alina stared. "Mom! You lied?"

Her mother shrugged. "I reasoned if he was forced to spend a night in my company, he would no longer think of me as just another girl to be taken for granted." She smiled, the smug look of a cat on a silk cushion. "And I was right."

"I'm not going to do something like that with Marty," Alina said. Especially when Eric was the only man she really wanted. "What if Grandma was wrong?"

"Your grandmother was never wrong!" The idea clearly horrified her. "Besides, don't you know I inherited a little of her gift also?"

"What do you mean? You've never told me you could predict the future."

"I can't. After all, I'm only one-quarter Romany. But I sense things. And I sense that this young man—this Marty—is important to you. He's going to be the one to make you happy."

Alina's spirits sank. Why did everyone know these things but her?

Eric returned to the table, effectively ending their conversation. Her father put away the trail map. "Tell me about Thanksgiving," he said.

"What would you like to know?" Eric asked.

"I want to write a paper," her father explained. "I study social customs and traditions at the university. I want to know all about this American holiday."

Eric glanced at Alina. "I'm not sure where to begin. There were some pilgrims and some Indians, and they had this feast…"

"Yes, yes, that I know from my research." He waved

away Eric's clumsy history lesson. "I want you to tell me how people go about celebrating. What do they do to show they're thankful?"

"Um, mainly eat a lot. And watch football. And…get together with family and friends." He cleared his throat. "I'm not explaining it very well, but it really is about getting together and celebrating family and tradition and lots of good food."

Mr. Allinova nodded. "I am trying to talk Alina's mother into preparing a traditional American Thanksgiving feast while we're here."

"Mom, that's a lot of work," Alina said, picturing her apartment kitchen in chaos. "I thought we'd go to a restaurant to eat."

"That's not very traditional," Eric said. "You should come to my house."

"Oh, I don't know…" Alina demurred, uncertain how Eric's family would respond to her mom and dad and vice versa.

"Yes! A typical American Thanksgiving," Alina's dad said.

"My mom fixes a big meal, and even with all my brothers and sisters and their families, there's always plenty of leftovers," Eric said. "She'd love to have you."

"We would not want to impose," Alina's mother said.

"Trust me, we always have extra people. The guy you just met—Marty? He'll be there."

Mrs. Allinova's eyes sparkled. She gave Alina a knowing look and nodded. "Then we will certainly be there."

Chapter Nine

"How'd it go with Alina's parents yesterday?" Marty asked when he met Eric and John, Eric's brother, the next morning. Their plan was to check out some back-country terrain that had reportedly gotten good snow in a recent storm.

"Whoa! You met Alina's parents?" John froze in the act of lacing up his snowboard boots and stared at Eric. "Alina Allinova?"

"Her mom and dad are visiting from Croatia and I got them some lift tickets," Eric said. He adjusted the strap on his helmet. "You guys ready to go?" Without waiting for an answer, he shouldered his skis and started up the steep trail up a rocky ridge.

Grumbling only a little, the others fell in behind. Eric hoped this would be the end of the discussion of Alina or her parents, but he should have known John wouldn't drop it. The first break they took to rest, John moved up alongside him. "Meeting the parents—that sounds serious, *hermano*," he said.

"They're visiting Alina and they like to ski, that's all,"

Eric said. And that was all, at least as far as Mr. and Mrs. Allinova were concerned. His feelings for Alina were another matter—a private one.

"You two have been seeing a lot of each other, though, haven't you?" Marty asked as he joined the other two in leaning against an outcropping of rock.

"We're friends," Eric said.

"Friends? What kind of friends?" John nudged him. "Friends with benefits?"

Eric slugged his brother in the shoulder. "Shut up and climb."

They climbed. The trail becoming progressively steeper, the only sound the squeak of snow beneath their boots and the huff of their breath as they labored in the thin air. Patches of brown earth and gray granite showed through the snow in places, like the surface of a cake too thinly frosted.

"I don't know about this," Marty said when they finally stopped at the top of the ridge. He frowned at the rugged terrain stretched out before him. "It looks iffy."

Eric stepped into his skis. "We can ski it," he said.

"Not as much snow as I'd like," John agreed.

"No guts, no glory," Eric called as he shoved off down the narrow line he'd scouted out. He winced as gravel scraped against his skis, and threw his body into a hard right turn. This was what he lived for—these moments when every part of his being was focused on the task at hand, so present and aware and *alive*.

He planted his pole as his skis skittered on a slick of ice, and felt the adrenaline rush as he overbalanced and wavered, the slope below looming up before him, rocks and trees and thin air beckoning. Threatening.

With a grunt, he hauled himself upright and his skis found purchase. He slid to safety and turned to look back up the slope and waved. "It's great!" he called.

John shouted down a word their mother would have washed his mouth out with soap for, and started climbing down the slope, while Marty carefully maneuvered down in a series of tight sliding turns on his snowboard.

"You're crazy," Marty said cheerfully when he stopped alongside Eric.

"Obviously I got all the brains in the family," John said when he joined them.

"I got brains and looks," Eric said. "And balls." Not giving the others a chance to catch their breaths, he skied down a short, smooth slope and launched himself off a large boulder, shouting for joy as he sailed through empty air before landing in an explosion of soft, fresh snow at the bottom.

"Idiot!" John shouted just before he followed Eric off the boulder, almost landing on top of him.

Marty chose to slide around the obstacle, skidding gracefully to a stop beside the brothers a moment later.

"Man, you are crazy," John said, laughing. "I should know better than to come out here with you. If Alina knows what's good for her, she'll stay far away from you. You might pass on these crazy genes to her children."

"Give it a rest," Eric snapped. "And keep your mouth shut around Alina."

"Hey, why are you mad at me?" John raised his hands as if to ward off a blow. Then he leaned closer to Eric, his expression somber. "I want to know, bro. Are you serious about this girl?"

Eric looked away, his heart pounding. He tried to tell himself it was just the aftereffects of the adrenaline rush of the jump, but he knew better. "I don't know. I really like her."

John kicked at a chunk of snow. "She seems like a nice girl," he said. "But she's so different, you know?"

"What's wrong with different?"

"Nothing if all you want to do is date her. But if you want to marry her…better to find someone from the same background. Someone who really knows where you're coming from."

"Who said anything about marriage?"

"Alina's only in the United States until January," Marty said. He sent Eric a sharp look. "Eric wouldn't lead on a girl when there's really no hope of a future."

"Who said anything about leading her on?" Eric protested. "Alina and I are friends, that's all. In fact, her mother kept asking me about *you*."

Marty looked surprised. "About me?"

"Yeah. She wanted to know all about what you did, where you were from, if you were seeing anyone." All the questions had annoyed him, though he thought he'd done a pretty good job of hiding his irritation. "I think she wants to set you up with Alina." What was it with matchmaking mothers? Why couldn't they let their sons and daughters find their own mates?

Marty shook his head. "Alina's a nice girl, but I'm not interested in dating her."

"Why not? Don't you think she's pretty enough?" The question came out sharper than Eric intended.

"She's really pretty," Marty said.

"And she's smart," Eric added.

"Why are you getting all upset with me?" Marty asked. "Alina's a great girl, she's just not my type."

"What do you mean, not your type?" How could any guy not want to be with someone like Alina? She was pretty and sweet and smart and—

Marty shrugged. "No spark."

Whereas Eric and Alina had plenty of spark. It was a wonder they didn't set fires they had so much spark. He looked away from his friend and met John's curious gaze. "Alina and her parents are coming to our house for Thanksgiving," Eric said. Let his brother try to make something of that.

"Her parents are coming, too?" John asked.

"Her father is some kind of sociology professor and he wants to write a paper on a typical American Thanksgiving."

John laughed. "So you invited them to our house?"

"Why not? Mom always makes enough food to feed an army."

"You don't think the molé and the piñata are atypical?"

"We have turkey and all the other stuff. And we're as American as anyone."

John nodded. "I guess so—to a Croatian."

"You were good to invite them," Marty said. "Us strays need a place to go Thanksgiving, and your mom loves making a fuss over everyone."

"Yeah, my little brother, the humanitarian," John

said. He nudged Eric. "Do yourself a favor and make sure Mama knows Alina is headed back to Croatia in a few weeks."

"Why should I do that?"

"She's worried you're serious about this girl."

"Why should that bother her?"

"She's Mom—she worries. She thinks a husband and wife ought to have more in common than physical attraction."

Alina and he did have more in common than physical attraction. They could talk about anything. They both liked the outdoors. They had the same sense of humor. "What do *you* think?" he asked John.

"I think Mom and Dad have been married for thirty-six years—maybe they know a thing or two about how to do it right."

Eric turned away. He couldn't argue with that logic. From the time he'd been old enough to think about what his future would be like, he'd wanted to emulate his parents—the loving marriage, the happy family, the place in the community. He wanted all those things.

But he wanted Alina, too. Knowing he couldn't have her hurt worse than any fall from these rocks ever could.

"WHAT ARE YOU GOING TO DO today while I'm at work?" Alina asked her mother the Tuesday before Thanksgiving. So far, Mrs. Allinova had spent the days while Alina was away reorganizing the kitchen so that Alina could no longer find anything. Her mother had cleaned, cooked elaborate meals and rearranged all the furniture. Her father had spent his days watching American television and scrutinizing the newspaper.

"I'm going shopping," Mrs. Allinova announced. "I want some new American clothes to wear to dinner Thursday."

"That's great, Mom. Do you want to borrow my car?"

"No. I am going with Mrs. Nelson."

"Mrs. Nelson?"

"Your neighbor downstairs. A very nice lady. I met her while I was doing your laundry."

Alina didn't even know she had a Mrs. Nelson as a neighbor. Leave it to her mom to make friends wherever she was. "That's great, Mom." She turned to her father. "What are you going to do, Dad?"

"I'm going to the History Museum, then I'm going to watch my shows."

His shows, Alina had discovered, were all the afternoon talk shows, from *Oprah* to *Dr. Phil* to people Alina had never heard of. Her dad was addicted, though he explained his fascination as merely the interest of a scholar of human behavior. "That's great," she said. She kissed him and then her mom. "Have a good day."

"I'll have dinner ready for you when you get home."

"Mom, you know you don't have to cook for me. We could go out."

"I know, but I want to." She patted Alina's cheek. "It makes me feel good to take care of my little girl again."

Alina could admit that it felt good to be taken care of sometimes, but maybe that was only because she knew it was temporary. In another ten days, her parents would return to Croatia and she'd resume her independent life here—a life it pained her to think of giving up in January.

Coming to America had been a big step, one she'd questioned at times. But now that her experiment in living on her own was almost over, she was reluctant to give up the freedom she'd found. Low wages and the high cost of housing made the possibility of living on her own in Croatia slim, not to mention that if she tried to move out of her parents' apartment, her mother might very well move into hers. The youngest daughter was still the baby in a Croatian family until she married.

Marriage. That was what Alina had really come to the United States to find, and so far she'd failed. Instead of the life partner she'd been looking for, she'd fallen for a dark-haired daredevil whose plans didn't include settling down for many years yet. She didn't want to give him up, but she didn't see the relationship moving forward, either. *Baka* Fania was probably shaking her head in disapproval over her granddaughter's perverse choice. "Do not plant pumpkins where they never sprouted," she would say, quoting a Croatian proverb. *Don't insist on doing something that isn't going to work.*

Alina's job provided a welcome distraction from her personal worries. Flu season had arrived, bringing with it bronchitis, pneumonia and a host of other ailments, and her services as a respiratory therapist were more in demand than ever.

Soon after arriving at work that morning, Alina was so preoccupied with a long list of patients to be seen that she almost didn't notice the woman seated outside the door of one of the rooms. Alina actually rushed passed her, then some spark of recognition made her back up and look at the woman again.

"Mrs. Herrera! What are you doing here?"

The older woman offered a weary smile. "Arturo is scheduled for surgery tomorrow. The doctor's examining him now."

Alina squatted down beside the chair so that Mrs. Herrera didn't have to crane her neck to look up. "I'm so sorry to hear that. Is it very serious?"

Mrs. Herrera nodded. "They're going to amputate his leg. Below the knee." She sighed, an empty, hollow sound. "The diabetes."

Alina hid her shock and patted the older woman's hand. "It is a terrible disease, and I'm sorry it's come to this. But it's good that his doctors are looking after him. And I'll be by to see him as soon as he's out of surgery to start his breathing treatments. I can come this afternoon if you think he needs me."

Mrs. Herrera shook her head. "He's breathing well, praise God." But this bit of good news did nothing to cheer her. "When he got the sores on his leg, I did everything the doctor told me. I followed all their instructions, but it got bad so fast…."

"Mrs. Herrera, this isn't your fault!" Alina gently squeezed the old woman's arm. "I've seen how you take care of your husband. You're the best nurse he could ever have. Things just happen this way sometimes."

"The doctor said that, too, but I can't help thinking if I'd done something different…"

"Please don't think that. Will you come walk with me a minute?"

Mrs. Herrera glanced at the door of the room behind her. "If the doctor needs to talk to me…"

"We won't go far. Just to the end of the hallway and back." She was getting a cramp from squatting down beside the chair, but more importantly, Mrs. Herrera needed a change of scenery and perspective.

"All right." Mrs. Herrera rose and allowed Alina to take her arm and lead her to the end of the hall, where a window afforded a view of a courtyard, the shrubberies and statuary frosted with snow.

"Tell me how you met your husband," Alina said.

"I wasn't supposed to meet him at all."

"You weren't?"

"No. I was supposed to meet his cousin, Sebastian. My school friend, Louisa, knew the family and she thought Sebastian would be perfect for me. So one Saturday afternoon, we drove out to their farm. We were taking some jars of pickled tomatillos Louisa's mother had made for the family, but really we were going to introduce me to Sebastian. Except Sebastian wasn't home."

Mrs. Herrera laughed, a surprising sound of mirth after the somber atmosphere of only moments before. "No one was home—except Arturo. The rest of the family had driven to Denver for the day, and Arturo had stayed to look after the livestock. Louisa was angry—she didn't like Arturo at all and didn't want me to meet him."

"Why didn't she like Arturo?"

"She said he was all wrong for me. Too wild and independent." Her smile transformed her face so that Alina had a sense of the beauty she had once been. "I was convent educated, from a prosperous family—very spoiled and sheltered. Arturo rode a motorcycle and smoked little cigarillos and had a job in the steel mills in Pueblo. He was so handsome—girls followed him everywhere. But he knew how good-looking he was and used it to his advantage." She laughed again, softer this time. "He really was all wrong for me, but the moment I laid eyes on him, none of that mattered. He was the only man I wanted. I wouldn't listen to Louisa or anyone else."

Alina listened, enthralled. She saw the dashing, dangerous man on the motorcycle, and felt the heart-pounding attraction of the quiet, sheltered girl for the handsome, daring man. Hadn't she had similar feelings for Eric? "I think he must have felt the same for you, no?" she prodded when Mrs. Herrera felt silent.

The old woman nodded. "He did, though he wasn't so willing to change his ways at first. He would ride up to see me on the weekends. The first time my parents met him, they forbid me to see him, but I would sneak out of the house to be with him. I lied to them and kept secrets, which I had never done before." She shook her head. "Love is like that sometimes," she said. "It makes you do crazy things. It made me crazy enough to confront him when I found out he was dating other girls during the week. I told him he had to choose. He either committed to me and no one else, or I wouldn't see him again."

"And he chose you."

Mrs. Herrera shook her head. "Not at first. Originally he was angry that I dared challenge him. He rode off on that motorcycle in a huff. I wept for a week. I wouldn't eat or sleep. My parents threatened to send me away to a convent." The smile returned. "And then he was back. He looked as if he'd been ill. He said he couldn't stop thinking about me, that he'd realized he would never be happy without me. We ran away together that night and were married."

"That's wonderful." Alina squeezed Mrs. Herrera's hands, unable to say more past the knot of tears in her throat. It was such a romantic story, and the outcome of the young couple's actions was so romantic, too—nine children, fifty-two years together, for richer, for poorer, in sickness and in health. They had been there for each other through a lifetime of troubles and happiness. It was all anyone could ask for—all Alina wanted.

"We'd better get back to the room," Mrs. Herrera said. "The doctor will want to speak to me."

"Of course." Impulsively, Alina hugged the older woman. "I'll stop by to see you later. Thank you for telling me your story."

"Thank you for listening, dear. It helped a little, remembering all Arturo and I went through to be together. It makes losing a leg seem like maybe not so much."

They walked down the hall together, and Alina left her friend at the door of the room and continued to the nurse's station.

"Hey, *chica*." Marissa sashayed to Alina's side. "Want to come to lunch with me? I'm celebrating."

"What are you celebrating?"

"Dr. Delicious and I had a very hot date last night."

Alina managed a smile for her friend. Marissa looked

particularly happy this morning, no doubt due to the attentions of the intern she'd been pursuing for the past several weeks. "I'd love to have lunch with you," she said, "but I don't think I have time." She gestured to the long list of patients on her clipboard.

"Just half an hour. We'll pop over to the Taco Hut for a quick bite. You can tell me how things are going with your parents."

"I love them, but they're driving me insane. My mother keeps rearranging my things, and my father analyzes everyone and everything as if we're all part of some big social experiment."

"See, you definitely need to vent about that kind of thing so you don't blow up at them at home."

Alina glanced at the schedule again. Most of the patients would be eating their own lunches, so she wouldn't be able to treat them during the noon hour anyway. She'd planned to use the time to catch up on paperwork, but the thought of escaping the confines of the hospital for even a few minutes to dish with Marissa was too tempting. "All right," she said. "But we have to make it quick."

They were waiting in line at the Taco Hut when a familiar feminine voice hailed them. "Marissa, Alina. Hello there."

Looking lovely and chic in pink yoga pants and matching hoodie, Sofia glided up to them. "Hey, Sofia," Marissa said. "What are you up to?"

"I had to take Eduardo his trumpet at school." She fluffed her abundant dark brown hair. "The boy would forget his head if it wasn't attached. Can I join you?"

"Of course." Alina moved over to make room for Eric's sister beside her in the booth.

"I hear you and your family are coming to our house for Thanksgiving," Sofia said.

"Yes. We're looking forward to it. None of us have ever had a real Thanksgiving dinner."

"Prepare yourself. It can be a madhouse—kids running everywhere, television blaring, the men arguing over which football game to watch, the women arguing over whether the gravy should have giblets or not." She waved her hands. "It's fun, but chaotic."

"I'm sure it will be wonderful."

Sofia stabbed a straw into her drink and took a long pull. "I understand you and my brother have been seeing a lot of each other," she said, her voice casual.

Alina stiffened. Had Eric's family been spying on them? "Is there something wrong with that?" she asked.

"It would be nice to see him get serious about someone and settle down," Sofia said. "He's getting a little old to play superhero."

Alina allowed herself to be encouraged by this small expression of support. "I think perhaps your mother does not approve of me with Eric," she said.

"Oh, don't pay any attention to her." Sofia waved away the suggestion. "Eric's her baby, so of course she thinks she knows what's best for him. Mind you, she's never been wrong, but there's a first time for everything, right?" She leaned closer. "Secretly she'd be thrilled with any woman who could domesticate him."

Alina spent a few moments mentally translating *domesticate*. Eric didn't really strike her as a wild man who needed to be tamed, but maybe there was another meaning in English. "You know I'm going back to Croatia in January," she said.

"I wondered." Sofia sighed. "Then you're just another of my little brother's temporary flings. I really thought he seemed more serious about you."

Alina's heart beat so hard it hurt. Eric seemed more serious about her? What did Sofia mean? What had he done or said to make his sister believe this? Was it even true? "Eric is going to medical school in the fall," she said. "He will be too busy for a relationship." She couldn't bring herself to say *marriage* out loud.

"People do manage to go to medical school and be married," Sofia said.

"Joey has lots of married friends," Marissa said. "Joey's an intern I'm dating," she explained to Sofia.

"It doesn't matter," Alina said. "I have to return to Croatia when my visa expires in January."

"You could get another visa," Marissa said. "Or Eric could move to Croatia for a while. He could even go to medical school there."

"Wouldn't my mother have a fit over that," Sofia said. She settled her chin in her hand and looked thoughtful. "Then again, it is so romantic—true love overcoming every obstacle."

Alina shifted in her chair. The picture of her and Eric as fated lovers meant to be together was too attractive to contemplate long. The idea was so sweet and seductive it threatened to overwhelm all the practical reasons the two of them shouldn't plan a future together.

Wanting something terribly couldn't make it come to

pass, any more than her grandmother's predictions could make Alina fall for a mysterious blond man when the only one she wanted was Eric. Their situation was hopeless, and the sooner she accepted that, the better.

Chapter Ten

Thanksgiving at the Sepulveda house revolved around the three Fs—family, feasting and football. The large kitchen at the back of the house was holiday central, where Mrs. Sepulveda and her daughters and daughters-in-law prepared for the feast like generals launching an enemy invasion. Eric played the role of dutiful son, and stuck his head in the doorway long enough to say hello to his mother and offer to help.

"The last thing we need is you stumbling around underfoot," Sofia said. She was up to her wrists in bread-crumbs and chopped celery.

"Thank you for offering, son, but I think we're fine," Mrs. Sepulveda said, not looking up from the massive turkey she was basting.

Eric prepared to make a hasty retreat to the family room, where his parents' new flat-screen TV was tuned to the first of a marathon of football games, but before he'd cleared the doorway, his mother called after him. "When are Marty's friend Alina and her family arriving?" she asked.

Eric frowned. "Alina is my friend, too, Mom," he said.

Mrs. Sepulveda ignored this. "When are they arriving?"

"I don't know. Soon, I expect."

"Make sure to introduce them to everyone and find them a comfortable place to sit," she said. "I want them to feel at home."

"Sure thing, Mom." Though how anyone who hadn't been born into the chaos of his big, noisy family could ever feel at home here he had no idea.

He squeezed past a clump of teenage cousins in the hallway, stepped carefully around Sofia's youngest boy, who was stretched out in the middle of the living room floor coloring, slipped past the dining room, where another group of female relatives worked to set the table, and made it safely to the family room, where he took the last vacant spot on the sofa, next to Bart.

"I heard your girlfriend and her family are coming for dinner," Bart said during the first commercial break.

Though the other men in the room pretended to be focused on the television, they'd all seen the same beer commercial a hundred times, and Eric knew they were intent on listening to his answer. Denial was his first instinct, but he couldn't bring himself to say the words. Instead he hedged. "Alina's parents are visiting from Croatia and wanted to experience a big American Thanksgiving."

"So she *is* your girlfriend." Bart punched his shoulder.

"Once she gets a look at this bunch, she's liable to run screaming all the way back to Croatia." John grinned from a recliner, where he was stretched out with his oldest boy, Marcus, in his lap.

"We're not so bad." Eric winced at the sound of a crash, followed by a torrent of curses in Spanish from a female voice. The other men didn't even blink; they'd learned long ago to pretend ignorance until they were called to the table. Their job on Thanksgiving was to stay quiet and keep out of the way. "Besides, Alina has met most of us before."

"And we've seen her," Bart agreed. "She's a pretty girl."

"Makes me wonder what she sees in *you*," John said.

Eric launched a pillow at his brother, but his uncle Henry intercepted it. "Some of us are trying to watch the game," he said sternly.

Eric tried to concentrate on football, too, but half his attention was on the other rooms, listening for Alina's arrival.

He knew the moment she walked in; several of the women and children rushed past the family room door, talking in excited whispers. Then he heard Marty's booming voice, followed by Alina's quieter one and the softly accented speech of her mother and father.

Eric bolted from the sofa and hurried to greet them. "Welcome," he said, pushing through the clot of relatives gathered around the front door. "Let me help you with your coat."

But Marty was already there, playing the gentleman, while Sofia and Cari assisted her parents with their wraps.

"I brought *makovnjaca*—poppy seed cake." Mrs. Allinova held out a red-and-gold gift bag. "From Croatia."

"How thoughtful of you." Sofia snatched the bag before Eric could even look inside.

"Did you have any trouble finding the house?" Cari asked.

"Marty was kind enough to come to Alina's apartment and pick us up." Mrs. Allinova beamed at the blonde.

Marty shoved his hands in his pockets. "I didn't mind," he said.

"I'd have picked you up if I'd known you needed a ride," Eric said.

"We knew you'd be busy with your family," Mrs. Allinova said. "And Marty was coming anyway."

"*I* would have driven," Alina said. "But Mother insisted on calling Marty." She frowned at her mother, who pretended not to notice her daughter's disapproving look.

"Come in, come in." Sofia took Mr. Allinova's arm and tugged him farther into the living room. "Dinner is almost ready." She looked around the room and spotted Eric. "Why don't you show Mr. Allinova to the family room," she said. "He'll want to watch the game with the other men. Us girls will stay in here and get to know each other."

Eric didn't want to rejoin the other men now that Alina was here, and he was pretty sure Sofia knew it. She pretended not to notice him glaring at her.

"What game are we watching?" Mr. Allinova asked.

"Football," Marty said. "It's tradition to watch football on Thanksgiving."

"Tradition?" Mr. Allinova's expression sharpened to one of interest. "Then I must certainly participate."

"Marty can show you to the family room, Mr. Allinova," Eric said. "I'll show Alina where she can stash her and her mom's purses." Without waiting for an answer, he took Alina by the arm and led her toward the back bedroom where coats, hats, gloves, purses and backpacks were piled like leftovers from a rummage sale. He pulled her inside, shut the door behind them and kissed her soundly.

Alina stiffened, then relaxed in his arms. She slid her hands up his chest, up his neck and into his hair, cradling his head, pulling him firmly toward her, lips together, tongues entwined. When they finally came up for air, they grinned at each other with dazed expressions. "It seems like forever since we've had a minute alone," he said.

"Since my parents arrived," she said. "I've missed you."

"I've missed you, too." He smoothed back her hair. "I'm glad you could be here today."

"I'm glad to be here. My parents will enjoy it, and it will be nice for them to have someone besides me to focus on."

"I guess it's been a little intense, huh?"

She rolled her eyes. "I love them both, but I'd forgotten how smothering they can be. I can't leave the house without being interrogated by my dad about everything from where I'm going to when was the last time I changed the oil in my car. And my mom is constantly cooking, cleaning or offering me advice."

He laughed. "That's what parents do."

"Yes, but I'd forgotten how *constantly* they do it." She glanced over his shoulder. "Maybe we'd better go out there, or everyone will start to wonder what we're doing in here."

"Let them wonder." He pulled her close once more, and she didn't hesitate to return his ardor. There would be plenty of time to subject her to his family later. For now he would make the most of these precious minutes to themselves.

IN SOME WAYS Thanksgiving dinner with the Sepulvedas was like any other feast day in Croatia. There were the same tables heaped with specialties associated with the holiday, the same crowds of family and friends, the same petty squabbles over the right way to carve the main course or prepare a special side dish, and the same atmosphere heavy with memories of every such feast day that had gone before.

At the meal, Alina found herself seated between Marty and her father, with Eric's brother Bart across from her, though she could barely see him around a footed bowl heaped with mashed potatoes. A large turkey took pride of place at one end of the long table, with a ham at the other. Other bowls held green beans, pinto beans, rice, sweet potatoes and other dishes Alina couldn't name.

"Try the chorizo and cornbread dressing," Mrs. Sepulveda urged, passing the baking dish to Mr. Allinova. "And try the green chili corn and the mole sauce for the turkey."

"Everything looks wonderful," Mrs. Allinova said. She'd spotted the plate of *makovnjaca* near the turkey, and Alina knew she was satisfied she'd made a suitable contribution to the meal.

"What is the significance of the turkey?" Mr. Allinova asked as he accepted a large slice of the bird.

"The pilgrims supposedly ate turkey at the first

Thanksgiving," Eric said. He was seated farther down the table, next to his grandmother.

"The Indians probably had to hunt it for them," Bart said.

"I hear they ate eels, too," one of the cousins said.

"They probably didn't eat mole, but we do," John said. "And we don't eat eels."

"Some of the old, some of the new—that's how families form their own traditions," Mr. Sepulveda said.

"It is always good to honor tradition," Mrs. Allinova said. "Young people can learn a lot from the old ways."

"This is so true!" Mrs. Sepulveda held up a serving spoon like a scepter. "All this talk of independence and doing things their own way, when all along they want the same things we wanted and our parents before us wanted—home and family, health and happiness. Those of us who were fortunate enough to enjoy all these things want to pass the lessons we learned on to our children."

"Exactly!" Mrs. Allinova leaned forward, her face flushed with triumph. "Why should a person make things difficult and start from scratch, when if they only listened to us, we could tell them all they need to know to find the happiness they look for."

"Of course we listen to you, Mom," John said. "Even when you think we aren't paying attention, we listen."

"Yes, you listen eventually," Mrs. Sepulveda conceded. "Though some of you take longer to absorb what you've heard." She looked down the table toward Eric.

Alina's face felt hot, aware that so many eyes were fixed on her—including her mother's. She wanted to protest that there was nothing wrong with being your own person and making up your own mind, but feared this would only launch her mother into a recitation of the list of every bad decision Alina had ever made, from the time she decided to cut her own hair when she was six to the car she'd bought against her father's best judgment. The car had died and left her stranded in a rainstorm one night, and by the time she walked home she was drenched and thoroughly repentant.

If you can't even choose the right car on your own, how can you possibly decide on something as important as the man you'll spend the rest of your life with? a voice uncomfortably like her mother's spoke inside her head.

Alina shifted her gaze to her left, to where Marty was demolishing a mountain of food. Ever since she'd met the big blond man, Alina's mother had been finding ways to bring him and Alina together. Clearly she thought Marty was the man from *Baka* Fania's prophecy.

Marty seemed oblivious to her mother's manipulations and to the tense conversation taking place practically in his lap. When he saw Alina watching him, he smiled and swallowed. "What do you think so far?" he asked.

"Think?" About her mother's interference? About Eric? About *him?*

"About the dinner. Your first Thanksgiving."

"Oh, it's very good. Thank you for asking." She focused on cutting her turkey into tinier and tinier pieces. The food was very good; too bad she was too nervous to eat it.

"Mom, you talk about tradition, and I agree that's im-

portant, but you aren't afraid to do things differently."
Sofia smiled at Alina and her parents. "Having a piñata
at Thanksgiving isn't traditional, but we've had one ever
since I was a little girl."

"It keeps the little ones occupied while we clean up
after the meal," Mrs. Sepulveda said.

"See, Mom—it's smart to try new things sometimes," Eric said.

Mrs. Sepulveda looked ready to argue, but John effectively distracted her. "What kind of piñata did you
get this year?" he asked.

"It's a turkey. Very big with brown and gold
feathers." She spread her arms to show the size. "It
took up the whole backseat on the way home from the
store."

"I would have liked to have seen a cop's face if you
got stopped," Bart said.

"Why would that happen?" Mrs. Sepulveda asked. "I
never drive too fast—not like some." She sent Eric another pointed look.

"Mom, I don't drive too fast," Eric protested. "I
mean, not usually."

"You are too reckless. You should listen to your
mother and settle down."

Eric and Alina exchanged glances. She was the first
to look away, not wanting to reveal too much. All this
talk of family and traditions, coupled with the memories of feast days growing up, had left her confused
and out of sorts.

After dessert of pecan and pumpkin pie and her
mother's poppy seed cake, everyone helped to clear the

table. The younger children, who had eaten at a long table in another room, supervised by two of the older girl cousins, had already finished their meal and raced into the backyard, where they surrounded a tree from which hung a big brown blob.

"Leave the dishes." Eric took Alina by the arm. "You have to see this."

He led her into the yard, and they watched as Eric's father climbed a stepladder and removed the brown paper covering a large papier-mâché turkey. The children cheered and clapped, and Alina joined in the applause.

"Watch what happens next." Eric put his arm around her and leaned in close. Sinking into his embrace would be the easiest thing in the world to do, but she wasn't doing either of them any favors by continuing to give in to temptation.

"Enrique, you come here. You go first." Cari beckoned one of the younger cousins and fastened a blindfold around the child's eyes. Mr. Sepulveda handed Enrique what looked like a length of broom handle.

"Ready, set, go!" Cari cried.

Enrique slashed at the air with the broomstick, narrowly missing one of the other children.

"That looks dangerous," Alina whispered.

"That's one of the things that makes it so much fun," Eric said, laughter in his voice.

Eric's father and brother took turns operating the rope that raised and lowered the piñata. The bright paper turkey danced in the air as the children took turns wearing the blindfold and swinging at it.

Finally one of the older children made contact. Another cheer rose as a gash appeared in the piñata's side. The blows came faster now, and soon the turkey hemorrhaged, spilling a shower of small gifts. The children dove to gather the booty, while the adults played referee and made sure that every child had some part of the prize.

"What's in it?" Alina asked.

"Some candy, but mostly little knickknacks Mom and my sisters buy at party stores or off the Internet," Eric said. "Cheap stuff the kids will play with for a while. Like Mom said, it keeps them out of the adults' hair while we clean the kitchen and watch the game or nap."

"What do you usually do after the meal and the piñata?" she asked.

"All of the above." He slipped his hand into hers. "But maybe I'll start a new tradition this year."

"Oh?" She avoided looking at him, afraid of the power he had to weaken her resolve to do the *right* thing. "What is that?"

"No one will notice if we go back to the coat room for a while."

She pulled her hand from his. "I don't think we'd better do that," she said.

"Why not?"

"Because everyone is watching us."

"The saying in my family is that if you don't do something for them to talk about, they'll make something up." He grinned and pulled her close again. "If they're going to gossip about us, we might as well enjoy it."

She laughed and pushed him away again. "I should help your mother in the kitchen."

He sighed and surrendered. "I guess so. But be careful—it's a war zone in there."

Though Alina had never been on a battlefield, she thought the Sepulveda kitchen more closely resembled the aftermath of a tornado. Dirty plates, pots and pans and dishes of leftovers occupied every flat surface. At least a dozen women jostled back and forth, scraping plates, rinsing pots and stowing leftovers. Alina spotted her mother at the sink, chattering away with another older woman who might have been Eric's aunt.

"Can I do anything to help?" Alina asked.

At least half the women in the room turned to look at her. Mrs. Sepulveda wiped her hands on her apron and shook her head. "Thank you for offering, but you are my guest. Go, enjoy yourself."

"I really want to help." She snagged a dish towel from a hook by the sink. "I can help dry the dishes." No one would be able to say later that she hadn't done her fair share of the work.

"It really isn't necessary." Mrs. Sepulveda turned back to the sink. "But suit yourself."

"The dinner was so delicious," Alina said. "I'd love to have your recipe for the dressing."

"I don't really have it written down. It's the kind of thing a girl learns standing at her mother's elbow, helping to prepare the meal year after year."

"And even then, some of us don't know it," Sofia said.

"We have recipes like that in our family, too," Alina's mother said. She sighed. "It makes me sad to think of all the things my mother made that I never bothered to write down. Now they are gone forever."

"So many young women don't cook these days," Mrs. Sepulveda said.

"That's true," Mrs. Allinova agreed. "But Alina is a good cook. Better than me, even."

"The man who marries her will be lucky," Sofia said, a teasing glint in her eyes.

"That Marty will need a wife who can cook," Mrs. Sepulveda said. "He's a big man with a big appetite."

Marty again. It was enough to make Alina scream. How could she let Eric's mother know that she wasn't interested in Marty—but in Eric? She opened her mouth to say as much, but her mother interrupted.

"Marty is such a nice young man," Mrs. Allinova said. "So polite and thoughtful and studious and…"

Boring, Alina thought. "You must be very proud of Eric." Alina interrupted her mother's cataloging of Marty's merits. "I understand he's applied to medical school."

"Of course I'm proud of all my children." Mrs. Sepulveda's gaze drilled into Alina, as if the young woman had suggested the opposite.

Alina gave up trying to make friends with the woman. Eric's mother had obviously made up her mind not to like her, for whatever reason.

She was silent for a while, drying dishes mechanically, determined to get through this time in the kitchen as quickly as possible.

Then Mrs. Sepulveda surprised her by addressing her. "Your friend Marissa seems like a very nice girl," she said.

"Yes, Marissa is very nice."

"Is she dating anyone in particular?"

Alina could see where this was headed. "She is dating someone," she said. "An intern at the hospital."

Mrs. Sepulveda frowned. "Is it serious?"

"I believe it is." As serious as Marissa ever got, considering how she flitted from man to man like a butterfly who couldn't choose one flower to stay with.

"Are they engaged?" Mrs. Sepulveda asked. "I didn't see a ring on her finger."

"No, they're not engaged," Alina admitted.

Mrs. Sepulveda smiled. "Good. She is exactly the sort of young woman I'd like to see Eric with."

"They would be perfect together," Mrs. Allinova said.

Alina glared at her mother, who pretended not to notice. "Eric may have someone different in mind," she said. *Maybe he loves me.* But she wasn't ready to say those words out loud.

"It's important for a young couple to have things in common," Mrs. Sepulveda said. "Family, friends, religion and traditions…"

"I agree," Mrs. Allinova said. "It makes things so much easier for them."

"Mother!" Alina protested. When the other women turned to stare at her, she flushed, but continued, "My older sister, Zora, married a man from Scotland, and they're very happy together."

Mrs. Allinova looked unmoved. "They were a rare case, obviously meant to be together." She turned to Mrs. Sepulveda. "I knew it the moment I saw the two of them together."

Mrs. Sepulveda nodded. "A mother knows these things."

"Just the way I knew that Alina and Marty would be happy together, from the moment I met him," Mrs. Allinova continued.

Alina wished she had the nerve to step on her mother's toes. Anything to make her shut up about Marty.

"I felt the same way." Mrs. Sepulveda's smile seemed genuine this time when she looked at Alina. "You and Marty fit so well together."

Alina twisted her dish towel into a knot. Why could everyone else see this great potential for her and Marty, when she couldn't?

"I think that's all the dishes," Sofia announced. She untied her apron and breathed a large sigh. "I'm ready to sit down and have a glass of wine."

"Me, too," several other women chorused.

"Thank you for your help," Mrs. Sepulveda said graciously. "Now we can all relax and enjoy the afternoon."

Alina didn't wait for more. She tossed aside the dish towel and hurried from the room, but not to find Marty. Instead, she wandered the now-deserted dining room and hallways, studying the family photos that lined the walls.

In several group shots, she found Eric amidst the crowd of children gathered around Mr. and Mrs. Sepulveda. As an impish six year old he grinned at the camera, the gap where one tooth was missing giving him a mischievous quality.

At thirteen he stood tall, obviously trying to appear grown-up and aloof. By seventeen, he'd returned to the smile of his childhood, though broad shoulders and handsome features left no doubt he was more man than boy.

Other photos showed Eric racing a dirt bike, posing next to a ski racing trophy, and dressed in his paramedic's uniform. In each one he appeared fearless and friendly.

"What are you doing?"

She looked over her shoulder to Eric, who stood in the doorway. "I'm looking at pictures of you," she said.

He joined her in front of the wall of photographs. "I look so goofy in some of these."

"No, you look sweet." She tucked her arm in his and leaned close. "I wish I'd been around to see you grow from a goofy boy to handsome man." Then she'd have been the girl from the neighborhood that his parents could have approved of.

"I bet you were a really cute little girl," he said. "I wish I'd known you then."

An image of her at thirteen, a period of frizzy hair, pimples and too much baby fat, flashed into her brain. She shook her head. "I'm glad you didn't know me then," she said. "It might have made you want to avoid me forever."

"I doubt that, but there is something to be said for keeping the past in the past." He wrapped his arms around her. "Or for discovering things about each other slowly. It makes it more…interesting."

"It does that." She thought of the female half of his family and hers in the kitchen, and the male half in the living room right next door. Any one of them was likely to walk in and discover them like this, necking shamelessly beside the remainders of the Thanksgiving feast. She'd be terribly embarrassed if they raised a fuss. She pulled away slightly.

"How did it go in the kitchen?" he asked.

She made a face. "Both your mother and mine said they thought Marty and I would make the perfect couple. And your mother said Marissa was exactly the kind of young woman she wanted for you."

"She said that? To your face?"

Alina nodded. Why hadn't she found the courage to speak up—to tell Mrs. Sepulveda that she wasn't interested in Marty. Why hadn't she insisted that she and Eric had more in common than his mother thought, and that they really cared about each other. "I guess I was too shocked to speak," Alina said. "All your relatives were there…I didn't want to ruin the holiday by arguing."

"I'll talk to her." Eric's expression was grim. He moved as if to go in search of his mother.

"No!" Alina clung to his arm. "Don't spoil the afternoon." Later she and Eric might have to face their parents, but for now that could wait. Thanksgiving was a holiday dedicated to being thankful. And right now she was thankful for Eric.

Chapter Eleven

Eric spent much of the next twelve hours thinking of all the things he should have said to Alina in those moments when they were alone after Thanksgiving dinner.

He should have told her he didn't care what his parents thought—that he was his own man and he knew she was the right woman for him.

He should have insisted that her parents would grow used to him in time. After all, wasn't he a nice guy?

He should have told her he loved her.

But he couldn't get the words out. Maybe it was the memory of Marty telling him not to lead her on, or the way both their parents thought she and Marty were a better match than she and Eric. Did their folks see something he didn't? Was it possible they were right when they said he and Alina didn't belong together?

What was he doing even worrying about a relationship right now? Hadn't he said all along he couldn't handle medical school and a woman at the same time? He still believed that, even if the woman was Alina.

"Earth to Eric!" Maddie leaned down and snapped her fingers in front of his face.

"What?" He looked up from his seat at a table in the EMS station ready room.

"You're doing it again," she said, hands on her hips.

"Doing what?"

"Spacing out on me. One minute we're talking, the next you're off in another world. What's the matter—didn't you get enough sleep last night?"

He hadn't slept well—thoughts and half-waking dreams of Alina and continuous replays of comments and reactions from both their families had kept him from slumber. "I'm okay," he said, turning away from her gaze.

"Still tired from the big Thanksgiving dinner?" Marty asked. He was seated in a recliner across the room, a theology book open on his lap.

"I almost forgot about that." Maddie slid into the chair across from Eric. "How did that go? The big meeting of the families?"

"It went fine," Eric said.

"Fine? That's all you can say?" Maddie turned to Marty. "What happened yesterday?"

Marty shrugged. "Lots of stuff. We all ate dinner, then most of the women helped out in the kitchen, while the men watched the game. The Buffs beat Nebraska. One of Sofia's little boys stuffed a bean up his nose because one of his cousins dared him to, and Sofia and I flushed saltwater up his nostrils for half an hour before the bean came out. Eric's mom and his sister Cari argued over whether to get a real Christmas tree or a fake one and how many lights to put on the house this year. John and Bart arm wrestled to see who got the last piece of pecan pie—John won."

Eric frowned. "It's a little freaky sometimes how you know my family almost as well as I do," he said. His mom and dad had welcomed Marty in as one of their own, so why couldn't they do the same for Alina? Eric couldn't understand why they believed that when it came to marriage, happiness lay with a mate whose background closely matched one's own.

"Forget the after-dinner play-by-play," Maddie said. "What did Alina's parents think?"

"Marty took them home," Eric said. "Ask him." Though he'd never admit it, it still galled him that his friend had been asked to chauffeur the Allinova family that afternoon. Eric had offered to drive them home himself, but Mrs. Allinova had insisted that Marty do the job, and Alina had given in to her mother's wishes, though reluctantly.

"They had a good time," Marty said. "Mr. Allinova says he's going to write a paper or something about Thanksgiving. Mrs. Allinova traded recipes with your mom."

"That's good," Eric said. Recipes meant they had gotten along okay. His mom didn't share cooking secrets with just anyone. "Did Alina say anything about me?" he asked.

"No. But then she didn't say much of anything. Her parents did most of the talking. Her mother invited me for dinner tonight, but I told her I had to work."

Eric's stomach hurt.

"Alina's mother invited *you* to dinner?" Maddie asked. "Why?"

"Because she thinks Marty is the perfect man for Alina," Eric said. He glared at his friend. "If you hadn't been scheduled to work would you have gone?"

"I don't know." Marty shifted in his chair. "Would you be mad at me if I did?"

"Why should I be angry?"

"Maybe because you're in love with the girl and *you* should be the one having dinner with her?" Maddie threw up her hands and gave him a "men are such idiots" look— a look he'd gotten from his sisters many times before.

"You don't have anything to worry about," Marty said. "I already told you I'm not interested in Alina that way."

"Have *you* told her *you're* interested in her 'that way'?" Maddie asked Eric.

"It's not that simple, okay?"

"You love her. Why is it so hard to tell her?" Maddie asked.

"There are…complications."

"Such as?" Maddie folded her arms across her chest, waiting.

Eric turned to Marty, silently pleading for a little help. Surely another guy would understand it wasn't easy to lay his heart on the line. But Marty merely looked puzzled. "What kind of complications?" he asked.

Eric shifted in his chair and tried to think of a way to dodge the question, but both Marty and Maddie pinned him with their stares. They weren't going to let him leave the room without some kind of answer. "Medical school is going to be tough enough without trying to manage a relationship—especially with my parents and hers objecting to the idea of us together."

"So you're getting opposition from both sides." Marty nodded sympathetically.

"If it was just our families not approving, I'd find a

way to stand up to them," Eric said. "I managed to deal with their objections to my going to medical school. But I can't screw up my chances to be a doctor." His shoulders sagged. "And Alina is leaving when her visa expires. She's going back to Croatia."

"They have planes that travel between here and there, you know," Maddie said. "Telephones, too. And e-mail and texting and…"

"Yeah, yeah, yeah." They made it sound easy, but a real commitment to another person was a big step. Life changing. What if he ignored all the advice from his family and he turned out to be wrong? What if he flunked out of medical school because she distracted him too much? Or what if all the pressure tore the two of them apart?

Maddie opened her mouth to say something, but the blare of the alarm tone silenced her. The three bolted from their chairs and headed toward the ambulance bay as details of the call sounded over the loudspeaker. "A six-year-old-girl in respiratory distress," the dispatcher said, and gave an address on the east side of town.

Marty was driving tonight, so Eric piled into the back of the ambulance, while Maddie rode up front with Marty. Eric welcomed the opportunity to stay busy, to keep his mind off Alina.

The child's mother, pale but calm, met them at the door, and led them to where the little girl sat on the sofa, eyes wide, chest heaving as she labored to breathe. "She's been doing so well," the mother said as Maddie knelt and began talking to the girl while Eric prepared to take her vitals. "I thought we could wait another week to refill her prescription. The medication is so expensive…"

"What medication does she normally take?" Eric asked as he clipped a pulse oxymeter onto the child's finger and put his stethoscope to her chest.

The mother rattled off the names of a couple of inhalers. Behind them Marty was already setting up the nebulizer. They'd start the breathing treatment on the way to the hospital and administer oxygen, while continuing to monitor the child's vital signs and oxygen levels.

He wondered if Alina was on duty. If so, she might be called to help treat this little girl. She was great with kids; his nieces and nephews had loved her.

At the hospital, he spotted Marissa. "Is Alina on duty?" he asked.

"No. She took a few days' vacation to spend with her folks."

"Have you talked to her?"

"Not since the day before Thanksgiving. Why?"

He shrugged. "No reason." Except she'd have been most likely to tell Marissa what she really thought of him and his family. He turned to leave before she could ask about the dinner. "I'd better run."

"I guess I'll see you at the tree lighting," Marissa said.

"The tree lighting?"

"The lighting of the Christmas tree in Crested Butte. I thought Alina told me you all were going."

"Oh, yeah." They'd made plans to attend the tree lighting together. He brightened at the thought. Her parents would be there, of course, but he and Alina would probably be able to steal some time alone.

"We got another call," Marty said. "Let's roll."

"See you at the tree lighting," Marissa said.

"Sure." He wanted to spend as much time as possible with Alina, while they still had the chance.

WHEN ALINA'S MOTHER HEARD about another American holiday tradition—that of shopping on Black Friday, the day after Thanksgiving—she announced that she and Alina would have to participate. "I have to get gifts for your sisters and their families and for your aunt Oksana and uncle Sandor and Mr. and Mrs. Tesler, who are watching our place for us while we're gone and—"

"Mom! Where are you going to put all this stuff?" Alina asked as her mother settled into the passenger seat of Alina's car and pulled a long list from her purse. "The airlines have weight limits, you know."

"I brought an extra suitcase. And the stores will ship things, won't they? Now, where should we go first?"

Alina's father had declined to participate in their excursion, preferring to remain at Alina's apartment, watching TV and eating the leftovers Mrs. Sepulveda had sent home with them.

At least fighting the holiday crowds and sparring with her mother over gifts would help take her mind off Eric, Alina reasoned. "I thought we could go to Crested Butte," she said. "They have a lot of cute little shops there."

"That sounds good," her mother said. "And we can stop at that coffee shop and buy another of those wonderful bear's paw pastries."

Alina found a parking space in the public lot behind the Chamber of Commerce, and she and her mother joined the throngs of shoppers flowing in and out of the stores along Elk Avenue. At a sports outfitter, Mrs. Allinova fingered a man's fleece jacket. "This would be nice for Marty," she said. "What size does he wear?"

"Mom! You are not going to give Marty a Christmas gift." Her face burned as several heads turned to see what the fuss was about. She forced herself to speak more softly. "You don't know him well enough."

"Of course I wouldn't give him a gift," Mrs. Allinova said. "But he's your friend. You should get him something, just in case."

"Just in case of what?" Did her mother think that between now and December 25, the scales would fall from their eyes and she and Marty would suddenly realize that they were each other's destiny?

"It's Christmas," her mother said serenely. "Anything can happen."

Alina guided her mother past the display of jackets. "No gifts for Marty," she said. "Let's stick to family."

Out on the sidewalk again, Alina spotted a cute blue cottage set back a little from the street. A sign over the door identified it as Pine Needles. "Let's go in there," she said.

The store was a wonderland of color and texture. Chunky skeins of wool in jewel-tone colors spilled out of bins along one wall, while cubbies on the opposite side of the store housed gossamer strands in soft pastels. A spinning wheel sat by the front window, next to a display of hand-knitted goods.

"Hello, I'm Rhiannon." The statuesque brunette who introduced herself looked more like a runway model than a yarn goods dealer, though she wore an intricately made hand-knit sweater. "Do you knit or crochet?" she asked.

Alina shook her head no. *Baka* Fania had tried to teach her to knit once, but Alina had proved all thumbs.

"I give classes," Rhiannon said. "And I also have other items for sale." She gestured to the display.

Alina's gaze lit on a shawl draped around the shoulders of a mannequin. The delicate garment looked as if it was woven of spun sugar, light and fluffy, in shades of pink ranging from shell to sunset. "This is gorgeous," she said, fingering the soft material.

"It's alpaca, wool and silk," Rhiannon said. "Very lightweight but also warm. I have a few other colors, if you're interested."

"*Baka* Fania would have loved this," Alina said to her mother.

Mrs. Allinova nodded. "She was like a cat that way, always finding the most comfortable, warm place in the house. And she loved beautiful things."

Rhiannon left to help another customer. Alina reluctantly turned away from the shawl. She had no one to buy such a fine gift for; her mother's tastes were much more practical and she had no need of such a thing for herself.

Mrs. Allinova picked up a pair of sheepskin slippers. "Your father would like these. His feet are always cold."

While her mother searched for the correct size, Alina flipped through a rack of sweaters. She stopped at a soft heathery blue number. The sweater would look great on Eric, the color highlighting his olive skin and dark eyes.

Resolutely, she turned away, and followed her mother to the cash register. "Do you remember the Christmas your aunt Berta gave everyone in the family slippers she had knit?" her mother asked.

"Yes—out of that awful green yarn that turned all our feet green." She laughed at the memory. "And how about the year Dad bought everyone backpacks because he thought we all needed to hike and become more fit."

Mrs. Allinova nodded. "We all complained so much the next year he gave everyone big pillows, saying all we wanted was to sit in comfort."

"And just to spite him, we all went on and on about how much we adored our new pillows," Alina finished the story.

The two women left the store and proceeded down the sidewalk. "*Baka* Fania always gave the best gifts," Alina said. "I remember the year she gave me the most beautiful doll, with a whole wardrobe of clothing she had made herself." There had been a gossamer-fine knit shawl, a silvery evening gown and even a little beaded evening bag.

"She bought good gifts because she could always see what people really wanted," Mrs. Allinova said as she and Alina pushed their way into a crowded boutique.

"I guess the rest of us didn't inherit that trait," Alina said, thinking of some unfortunate sweaters and a particularly ugly purse that had been among the gifts her mother had given her.

Fortunately the implied criticism sailed right over Mrs. Allinova's head. "My mother's talent was rare," she said. "It was said not one in a hundred seers could see as clearly as her."

"Didn't she ever make a mistake?"

"Never."

"Never?"

"Well…sometimes people might interpret what she

said wrong. For instance, she might tell them they would soon take a long journey. They'd take this to mean they were going to enjoy a wonderful vacation, but what she really meant was that business or a family emergency would require them to make a long trip. Of course, that's exactly what happened. She was always right."

If her grandmother was always right, then that must mean Alina's feelings for Eric were wrong. Why, then, did they feel so right?

"Look, there is the coffee shop." Mrs. Allinova pointed at Trish's place. "I must go in and have another bear's paw."

"Sure." A strong cup of coffee sounded good right now.

The door to the shop swung open as they headed up the walk. "Merry Christmas, ladies," said Zephyr.

Today he was dressed head-to-toe in green, the long stocking cap dangling past his waist. A string of bells around his waist jangled every time he moved. "That is an interesting costume," Mrs. Allinova said, eyeing him warily.

"I'm an elf," Zephyr said. "Spreading holiday cheer. Oh, I almost forgot." He pulled a candy cane from a holster at his hip. "Have a peppermint."

"Thank you." Alina accepted the candy. She had to bite the inside of her cheek to keep from laughing.

"Hello, Alina, Mrs. Allinova." Trish, who was also dressed in green with a Santa hat on her head, greeted them. "Are you finding any good sales?"

"Many wonderful sales," Mrs. Allinova said. "And we've only just begun. But first, I must have coffee and another of your wonderful bear paw pastries."

"Coming right up."

Zephyr sat at the table next to theirs. "Are you shopping for all the relatives back home in Croatia?" he asked.

"Yes, we are buying gifts for family." Mrs. Allinova studied him. "Where is your family?" she asked. "Do they live here?"

"My folks are all back east," Zephyr said. "Connecticut and New York. I'm sort of the black sheep of the family."

"Black sheep?" Mrs. Allinova looked at Alina, puzzled.

"It means one who is different from the rest," Alina explained. Zephyr was definitely different. Then again, some might say Alina was the black sheep of her own family since she'd decided to come to the United States, so far away from the rest of them.

"Why would you want to be a black sheep?" Mrs. Allinova asked. "Is your family bad? Did they mistreat you?"

"No, no!" Zephyr protested. "My folks are great. They're just not as creative as I am. They're into making money and keeping up appearances and all that."

"Obviously Zephyr isn't concerned with money or appearances." Trish patted the top of her boyfriend's head as she delivered the women's order.

"My family and I look at the world differently," Zephyr said. "Nothing wrong with that. We still love each other and everything."

"That is what is most important," Mrs. Allinova agreed.

The front door opened and Zephyr leaped to his feet. "Better do my job," he said. "Merry Christmas."

"Merry Christmas," Alina and her mother echoed.

While Zephyr was occupied greeting the couple who had just arrived, Mrs. Allinova leaned closer to her daughter and said, "Blond or not, I'm happy you aren't interested in that one."

Alina traced one finger around the rim of her coffee cup. "Mom, what if I don't fall in love with a blond man?" she asked.

Mrs. Allinova patted her daughter's hand. "You will," she said.

"But I've been looking for years and I haven't found any man who fit that description."

Her mother tilted her head. "Marty is a nice man," she said.

"Marty is boring. How can I fall in love with a boring man?" She folded her arms across her chest. "Besides, he's not interested in me."

"How do you know?"

"I know, Mom."

"Maybe he is only being polite because his friend is pursuing you."

"Eric is a nice guy," Alina said. "I really like him."

"He's very handsome, and I'm sure he's nice, but he's not the one for you."

"Because *Baka* Fania said so?"

"You were always her favorite. She would have never said anything to lead you wrong. You must know that."

Alina nodded glumly. She knew it, but she couldn't reconcile the thought of losing Eric with any kind of future happiness.

She didn't want to talk about the subject anymore.

"How many more gifts do you need to buy?" she asked. "Do you know what you want to get?"

"So many names. I need gifts for your sisters and their husbands and some of the grandchildren…."

Through a second cup of coffee and the rest of Mrs. Allinova's bear claw, they talked of gifts and relatives and all the preparations for the approaching holiday, with no mention at all of Alina's uncertain future.

They hit the shops again, Alina determined to remain cheerful and to enjoy her mother's company, but the task was more difficult than she'd anticipated. "What do you think of this for your sister Radinka?" her mother asked as they riffled the racks at yet another boutique.

Alina scarcely glanced at the sweater her mother held up for her inspection. "I'm sure she'll love it," she said.

"I wonder if it will fit her, though?" Mrs. Allinova held the sweater at arm's length and scrutinized it. "She's gotten very big since she had the baby. She and Josef are talking about having another one, you know?"

Great. By the time Alina had her own children, all the cousins would be too old for her babies to play with.

"I think I'd better stick with gloves or a scarf," her mother said. "It's not as if she can exchange something if it's the wrong size." She returned the sweater to the rack. "What do you want for Christmas?" she asked.

She wanted a visa that allowed her to stay in the United States. She liked her life here and the closer she drew to the time to return home, the more she realized how much she wanted to remain in Colorado. "You don't have to get me another present," she said. "Seeing you and Dad is the only gift I need."

"Nonsense. Tell me something you really want."

She wanted Eric. But she couldn't have him, any more than she could have a new visa. He'd made it clear he wouldn't combine medical school and love. "Whatever you want to get me will be fine, Mom," she said. What was another ugly sweater in her closet when the things she really desired were so far out of reach?

THE TREE LIGHTING CEREMONY in Crested Butte involved not one, but three trees. First was the large evergreen in front of the Chamber of Commerce at the crossroads where the Grump had been burned during Vinotok only a few weeks before. From there, the crowd, singing carols, progressed to a tree erected in front of the post office on Elk Avenue, where they were joined by Santa and his elves. Finally the group made its way to the end of Elk Avenue, where a smaller tree known as the Children's Tree was decorated by the younger members of the crowd.

In true Crested Butte style, participants were encouraged to wear costumes. By the time Eric arrived at the crossroads, the crowd overflowed with elves, fairies and men and women and children wearing reindeer antlers, Santa hats or both.

He searched for Alina, remembering the first time he'd seen her here in this very spot the night of the Vinotok play. From the beginning, he'd sensed she was someone special. If he'd known just how special, would he have had the good sense to stay away from her and save himself his current heartache?

Probably not, he decided.

And then he saw her. She was laughing at something, her mouth open, head thrown back, eyes crinkled up at the corners. He stopped breathing for a moment, staring at her, everything else fading around him as he watched her. She was so beautiful. So sweet and funny and sexy and...

And nothing was going to come of that kind of thinking, he reminded himself. He took a deep, steadying breath, and then noticed that Alina wasn't alone. Her parents were with her, of course, but so was Marty. The big blonde stood beside her. Close beside her.

Naturally, everyone was standing close in this crowd, but what was Marty doing with her anyway?

Eric pushed aside the hot flare of jealousy and worked his way over to them. "Hey, Eric." Marty greeted him warmly.

"Hello, Eric." Alina was more subdued, her eyes downcast, but maybe she was shy with her parents so nearby.

"Mr. and Mrs. Allinova." He nodded to the older couple. "Do they have Christmas trees like this is Croatia?"

"Not many," Mr. Allinova said. He looked at the tall blue spruce which had been strung with hundreds of colored lights. "It's considered an American custom, but it is starting to catch on in Croatia, especially with younger people."

"The main tree is the one at the post office," Eric said. "That one has all kinds of ornaments and garlands."

"I like this one with just the lights," Alina said. "Simple and beautiful."

Beautiful like you, he thought. Though she was anything but simple.

"Alina and I spent the day shopping," Mrs. Allinova said. "I bought lots of wonderful presents for everyone back home."

"That's nice," Eric said. He hated shopping, and usually waited until Christmas Eve to fill his Christmas list.

He was saved from having to make further conversation by the appearance of a dozen or more white-robed carolers singing, "O Come, All Ye Faithful."

As the carolers led the way down Elk Avenue, the crowd fell in behind them. Eric walked beside Alina, a few paces behind her parents, whose attention was focused on the spectacle of lights, glitter and garlands along Crested Butte's main street.

He glanced at Alina, who chose that moment to look his way. He tried to take her hand, but she pulled away. "What's wrong?" he asked.

She shook her head, still avoiding looking at him. "Nothing." But he could feel a change in her attitude, a distance between them that had nothing to do with physical proximity.

"Something's wrong," he said. "Tell me."

She raised her eyes to his at last. They were shiny with tears. "Us," she whispered. "We're wrong."

He stopped, the crowd jostling him as they surged around him. Alina stopped also. She stood with her head down, shoulders slumped. "We're not wrong," Eric said. The words came out in an angry rush.

Alina flinched. "Eric, please," she said. "Don't make this harder than it has to be."

"You're the one who's making this hard. How can you say we're wrong?" Though hadn't he had this same argument with himself for weeks now?

"Has anyone in your family ever chosen someone that wasn't a Mexican-American, like you?" she asked.

"I don't know. I don't know everyone in my family. Like you said, it's a big family."

"I have eyes," she said sadly. "Not one of your brothers or sisters is married to anyone from a different background. For my part, no one in my family has ever found love with someone unless my grandmother predicted it first."

He stared at her, hurt and confusion warring within. "What does your grandmother have to do with this?" he asked. "Didn't you tell me she'd died?"

"Yes. But before she died, she told me that I was destined to marry a blond man."

"A blonde—she told you that?"

Alina nodded. "She said a big, blond man held the key to my happiness. I know it sounds foolish to you. Americans are so modern—they don't believe in that sort of thing. But in my country, we do. And *Baka* Fania was never wrong. I will only be happy with a blond man."

"Are you saying you're unhappy with me?" He closed the gap between them, his chest almost touching hers, his eyes boring into hers. "That the time we've spent together—the nights we've spent together—you've been unhappy?"

"No." She put a hand to his chest. He wanted to throw his arms around her but resisted. "I love you, Eric," she said. "Part of me will never stop loving you. Right now, you make me very happy, but I have to think of the future. I want to remember you now, while things are so special between us. If we're not meant to be together in the future, there will only be trouble and pain if we try to force it."

He blinked, stunned. "You think we'd be unhappy in the future because of your grandmother's prediction?"

She nodded. "And because your family thinks we are too different to make things work." She looked away. "Maybe they are right. Maybe it's the same thing *Baka* Fania was saying, too. Look at us, Eric. You're going away to medical school, I'm leaving the country—the odds are against us. You must see that."

He wanted to tell her he wasn't afraid of the odds, that the odds didn't matter. But the words died on his lips. He knew they did make a difference.

He was too stunned to speak, too angry and hurt and confused. "I'm going to miss you," she said. Then she threw her arms around him and buried her face against his neck.

His arms encircled her, pulling her close. She felt so small in his embrace, as fragile as crystal, and far more precious. He cradled her head, her hair like silk sliding beneath his fingers, the floral scent of it wafting around him.

He kept his eyes closed, holding back the tears that stung behind his tightly shut lids.

"Goodbye, Eric," she whispered, and then she was gone, slipping out of his arms and disappearing into the crowd.

Chapter Twelve

Alina's parents returned to Croatia the Monday after Thanksgiving, leaving her feeling lonelier than ever. The holidays only made everything worse, reminding her that at this time of year she had no one.

What had she been thinking, breaking up with Eric? Why hadn't she let things run their course? In January, when she had to return to Croatia, she and Eric could have parted company then. That breakup wouldn't have hurt her any more than the pain she was suffering now, and she would have at least had the memory of a few more days with him.

But no, she'd had some crazy idea she'd spare them both if she broke things off now. *Idiot!*

But a girl could pace and berate herself only so long. Alina wasn't really the type to brood. When she'd despaired of finding a man in Croatia, she'd headed for the United States. Maybe her current dilemma required similar drastic action.

If *Baka* Fania were here, Alina had a good idea what her grandmother would advise her to do. Ignoring her grandmother's counsel had brought her only heartache; maybe it was time to follow tradition and do what her mother and grandmother wanted.

Heart in her throat, but determined not to back down, she flipped through her address book until she found the number her mother had recorded in her neat hand.

The phone rang five times, and Alina was just about to hang up when a groggy voice answered. "Hello?"

"Hello, Marty? This is Alina. I'm sorry if I woke you."

"That's okay. I was just taking a nap. I needed to get up anyway."

"How are you doing? Did you have a late night last night?" Alina asked.

"Yeah. A lot of calls. I don't know what it is about holiday weekends, but that's the way it always goes."

She wanted to ask if Eric had worked with him, but banished the idea. "My parents left this morning to fly back to Croatia," she said.

"That's good. Did you have a nice visit?"

"Yes, it was very nice."

"That's good."

Good. Nice. *Alina wanted to gag.* Any other person might have made a comment about her parents, or asked how Alina herself was doing. "My apartment seems really empty without them here," she said. "I know I'll get used to being on my own again, but right now I really miss them."

"That's too bad."

"Um, I was wondering if we could get together and grab a bite to eat or something," she said.

"Is Marissa working tonight?"

Marissa? What did Marissa have to do with anything? "I don't know what she's doing," she said. "I wanted to go out with you." Did she sound desperate? Well, maybe she was.

"What about Eric?"

So that was it—Marty was worried about betraying his friend. Relief surged through her. Marty wasn't dim, just a nice guy. "Eric and I aren't dating anymore," she said.

"You aren't? Why not?"

Because I'm a coward who's afraid of being hurt wasn't something she was ready to admit out loud. "It's a long story," she said. "We're still friends, but it wasn't going to work out."

"I thought you two really liked each other," Marty said.

We did. We do. "I really just thought it would be nice if you and I went out—as friends—and got to know each other better," she said. "That's all."

The silence that followed was so long Alina feared Marty had fallen back asleep. "Marty? Are you still there?"

"Yeah." He made a sound that might have been a sigh. "You're a really sweet girl," he said. "But I'm really not interested in you that way."

What way? As a friend? As a girlfriend? As a dinner companion?

"I just don't think we'd be a good match," he continued. "I'm really looking for someone from my church. I mean, considering my future profession, it seems like a good idea."

"I only asked you to dinner," she said, unable to hide her irritation.

"Well, yeah, but if you just split with Eric…I don't think it's a good idea. Thanks anyway."

"Yeah, thanks."

She hung up and began to pace again. Great. Now her supposed Mr. Perfect wasn't interested because she didn't go to his church—they didn't have *similar backgrounds*.

It was enough to make a girl want to run away and join the circus.

ON TUESDAY EVENING, Marty and Eric responded to a call involving a man who'd been injured while stringing Christmas lights. "He's over here." A harried woman, her hair in hot rollers, met them at the end of the driveway and ushered them to where the man lay, propped on a stack of patio cushions.

"I think I broke my leg," the man said, grimacing at his right leg, which was twisted beneath him.

"You're lucky you didn't break your neck," the woman said. She turned to Marty. "I told him to wait and let our son string the lights."

"If I waited on him, the lights wouldn't be up until Valentine's Day," the man said.

"Let's see what we have here." While Marty checked the man's blood pressure and pulse, Eric knelt and gingerly felt along the leg.

"Is he going to be all right?" The woman loomed over them.

"There's no bleeding or broken skin." Eric looked at the man. "Does anything else hurt besides the leg?"

"My ribs are a little banged up from where I slid down the roof, but the leg is the worst."

"We'd better splint it for transport," Eric told Marty.

"Is he going to be all right?" the woman asked again.

"He should be fine," Eric said. "The orthopedist will want an X ray of the leg. Depending on what that shows, you might even be able to take him home tonight."

"I'd better call the Milfords and tell them we won't make their party," she said.

"I didn't want to go to their party anyway," the man said. He addressed Eric. "Two of the most boring people you'll ever meet. All he talks about is his investments, and all she talks about is her most recent surgery. It's almost worth breaking a leg not to hear that."

"Roger! You didn't do this on purpose, did you?" The woman's eyes were wide with horror.

"No, I didn't. I'm just trying to look on the bright side."

"I don't know why you insisted on putting those lights up at all."

Still looking at Eric, the man said, "She wants to know why I put the lights up. I put them up because *she* wants them. She's worse than a kid about Christmas. I'm not going to be the one to ruin her holiday because we're the only house on the block without lights."

"*I* want them? What are you talking about? *You're* the one who makes such a fuss about the lights every year."

"Are you kidding? All I hear all season is 'Aren't the lights beautiful?' and 'I just love our lights' and 'Our house is the prettiest one on the block' and 'It wouldn't feel like Christmas without the lights.'" His voice rose to a pinched falsetto with each sentence.

His wife continued to stare at him. "I only made such a fuss because it seemed so important to you."

"You're kidding."

She shook her head.

"You mean, I've been hassling with all these lights every year when neither one of us really cares about them?"

To Eric's amazement, the woman began to cry, loud noisy sobs that shook her shoulders.

"Bonnie, what is it?" Roger tried to sit up, but Marty urged him back down.

"You could have been killed!" Bonnie wailed.

"He's going to be all right." Eric patted the weeping woman's shoulder awkwardly. "He's going to be just fine."

"Do you want to call your son and ask him to meet you at the hospital?" Marty handed Bonnie a packet of tissues from the supply they kept in the ambulance. "Then why don't you, um, freshen up and you can follow us there."

Bonnie blew her nose loudly and nodded. "Yes." She put one hand to her head and laughed. "I'd better take these curlers out, too. I'll be right back."

She raced to the house, and Eric and Marty finished loading Roger into the ambulance. "When I get home, I'm going to put all the lights in a box and give them to charity," he said. "Then maybe I'll buy her some sparkly piece of jewelry. She's worth it, don't you think, for try-ing to humor me all these years?"

They left Roger and Bonnie at Gunnison Valley Hos-pital and headed back toward the station. "What's this I hear about you and Alina breaking up?" Marty asked as Eric backed the ambulance into the bay.

Eric slammed on the brakes, throwing them both forward in their seats. "How did you know we broke up?" he asked.

"She told me."

"Alina told you? When?"

"She called me the other day." Marty looked away. The guy would make a terrible poker player.

Eric shut off the engine but remained in his seat. "Why did she call you?"

Marty sighed. "She asked me out to dinner."

The words hit Eric like a punch in the stomach. He felt like doubling over, though he remained sitting behind the wheel, frozen. Two days after saying goodbye to him, Alina was ready to start dating one of his best friends?

"I told her no," Marty hurried to add. "That I wasn't interested. To tell you the truth, I don't think she's interested in me that way, either. Maybe all she really wanted was to get together and talk about you. Yeah, I'm sure that's it."

Eric wished he could believe that. But he didn't know what to think about Alina—or about women in general—anymore.

"So why did you split up?" Marty asked.

"What did she tell you?"

"Not much. She said it was a long story and that things weren't going to work out."

"That's about it." He opened the door and climbed out.

"That can't be it." Marty followed him into the men's locker room. "You two are great together."

"I can't talk about it now." Eric began unbuttoning his uniform shirt. He wasn't sure he'd ever be able to talk about what had happened with Alina, to put into words all his mixed-up feelings. "I have to go or I'll be late to my nephew's play."

The second-grade classes of Gunnison Elementary School were performing an original holiday play, starring none other than Bertie Abellero—Sofia's eldest son. Eric arrived a few minutes before showtime, and joined Sofia and her husband, Guillermo, Mr. and Mrs. Sepulveda, John and Bart and their families, and at least a dozen other members of the Sepulveda and Abellero clan.

"Quite a cheering section," Eric said, looking around. "Do you think the other kids are jealous?"

"They're used to it," Sofia said. She sat back in the chair beside him. "Just think, one day we'll all be here to root for one of your children."

At one time he would have laughed off this suggestion, but now he only felt sad at the thought. Maybe he was more ready to settle down than he'd realized.

He was quiet during the play, thoughts of Alina and all the ways he wished their situations were different distracting him from the children's fumbling, sweet efforts. Somehow he managed to applaud and laugh in the right places, but his heart wasn't in it.

"What's bugging you?" Sofia asked as the second graders filed off stage and the third graders shuffled into position.

"Why do you think something's bugging me?"

"You might as well have a little black cloud over your head," she said. "I can feel the sadness from here. What happened? Something at work?"

He shook his head. He could deny anything was

wrong, but Sofia was plugged into a vast gossip network. She'd hear about his breakup with Alina sooner rather than later. "Alina broke it off with me," he said.

"Why did she do that?"

He slid low in the chair, legs stretched out in front of him. "I don't know." He glanced at her. "She said my family didn't approve of her."

Sofia frowned. "Mama and Grandmama don't like the idea of the two of you together," she said. "Daddy goes along with whatever Mama says. But *I* like Alina, and I liked seeing how happy you were with her."

"That's not all. Her parents aren't wild about me." He glanced toward the stage. The third graders were having trouble finding their places. "They have this crazy idea she's supposed to marry a blond guy because of some prediction her gypsy grandmother made."

Sofia studied him. "We could try bleaching your hair."

"Believe me, I've thought of that, but I don't think it would work."

"You're right. Your hair is so dark it would take a lot of bleach. You could end up bald."

"That's not what I mean. I mean, changing my hair color isn't going to change how our families feel about us."

"It seems to me the most important thing is how the two of you feel about each other."

"I'm not sure we know."

She patted his thigh. "Then maybe you'd better figure it out. Before it's too late."

DURING THE NEXT TWO WEEKS work provided a welcome respite from Alina's brooding. Flu and pneumonia, heart disease and broken bones caused by falls on slippery sidewalks or snow-covered ski slopes kept the hospital busy. Falling temperatures and nasty cold viruses caused an increase in respiratory ailments and Alina's services were needed more than ever.

Twelve days before Christmas, she was dismayed to see a familiar name on her roster of patients. "Mr. Herrerra, what are you doing back here?" she asked, forcing a smile and a cheerful note to her voice, though the old man's frail appearance shocked her. Never a large man, he had shrunken further, as if folding into himself. He looked childlike against the pile of pillows on which he was propped, oxygen cannulas fixed to his nostrils. He blinked at her with faded eyes.

"It's that anesthesia from surgery," he wheezed. "Makes it harder to breathe. My lungs still aren't right."

The mention of surgery made her glance down to the flattened sheet beneath his knee. He'd had a rough few weeks. "I'm here to help you with the breathing," she said, and gently helped him sit up so that she could administer a treatment.

They were almost finished when the door opened and Mrs. Herrera entered the room. She, too, looked smaller than before, her flowered blouse too large for her narrow shoulders, dark circles under her eyes. She nodded to Alina, but said nothing.

"Are you doing a little better?" Alina asked Mr. Herrera as she coiled the nebulizer tubing once more.

"A little," he nodded, and eased back onto the pile of pillows.

She adjusted the oxygen and checked the flow. "I'll

check on you again in a few hours, but if you need anything in the meantime, press the call button for the nurse."

He nodded, and Alina reluctantly turned to go. She wished she could stay here awhile, watching him, making sure he was okay, but she had a long list of other patients who needed her, as well.

Mrs. Herrera followed Alina into the corridor. "I apologize for not being there when you arrived," she said. "I stepped out to try to get warm."

"You're cold?" Alina asked.

The older woman nodded. "They keep the rooms here so cool. I guess because of all the equipment." She rubbed her arms. "I'm always cold anyway, especially now that I'm older."

"You should wear a heavy sweater or a shawl," Alina said.

"I should, but I keep forgetting to bring one." She glanced over her shoulder, toward the closed door behind which her husband lay. "He had a bad night last night."

Alina gave the older woman's shoulder a reassuring squeeze. "We'll do everything we can to help him."

Mrs. Herrera nodded, but her expression was still glum. "He's suffered so much."

"And you suffer with him," Alina said.

She nodded. "This will be our fifty-third Christmas together. All I want is for his pain to go away…and I worry what I would ever do without him."

Alina nodded, but could think of nothing to say. Mr. Herrera was very old and very sick, and his prognosis was grim.

Mrs. Herrera drew herself up taller and straightened her shoulders. "I know you're doing everything you can," she said. "And there's no sense worrying about what might happen. The important thing is to be with each other right now."

"Don't give up hope, Mrs. Herrera," Alina said. "The doctors are doing everything they can."

The older woman patted Alina's hand. "I know they are, dear. And anything could happen. After all, it's almost Christmas."

BEFORE RETURNING HOME to Croatia, Alina's mother had decorated her apartment for Christmas, right down to a little tree and a pile of wrapped presents. Alina's father had helped, as evidenced by the multiple screws anchoring the tree in its stand, and the instructions he had left behind that the tree was not, under any circumstances, to be left plugged in when she was not at home.

But decorations and presents did little to lessen the loneliness Alina felt as the holidays crept closer. This time last year, she'd been busy planning for her yearlong stay in the United States. There had been paperwork to complete and shopping to do, English to brush up on and a thousand admonishments from her parents to eat right, avoid riding with strangers, be sure to get enough rest and to remember to call home. Those days had been filled with excitement and anticipation of seeing new things and having new adventures. And always, underneath everything, had run the constant current of hope that this trip would lead to the biggest adventure of all: falling in love with the one man she was meant to be with, the man who was destined to bring her happiness and love.

So much for all those dreams. Nothing had gone the way she hoped. Yes, she had made friends and found a job she loved, but now she was going to be forced to leave them all behind. The patient to whom she'd grown closest, Mr. Herrera, was ill and might never get well, and Mrs. Herrera's heart was breaking while Alina was powerless to help her. There didn't seem to be much about the season worth celebrating.

On this grim thought, Alina switched off the lights on her tree and went into the kitchen. Maybe a cup of tea would make her feel better. She opened the drawer where she kept her tea bags and riffled through the selection. But instead of tea, she drew out the little plastic bag of wheat seeds her mother had brought from Croatia.

She traced a fingernail over the small oval kernels. As a child, Alina and her sisters had planted the wheat on December 13, St. Lucy's Day, in a dish kept just for this purpose.

Alina checked the calendar. Today was the fourteenth of December. It was already the fifteenth in Croatia—a bit late but close enough. She opened a cabinet and searched through her collection of mismatched dishes until she found what she was looking for: a wide, shallow soup tureen. Then she chose a big spoon and went through the apartment, scooping a spoonful of soil from each houseplant.

She built up a shallow layer of soil, and poked the wheat into it, then sprinkled it with water until it was moist but not soggy. She then set the dish in the middle of the kitchen table. By Christmas Day, the little stalks of wheat would be eight or nine inches tall. She would tie them with red, white, and blue ribbons—the colors of the Croatian flag—and place them near the Nativity scene.

As the youngest, Alina had always been allowed to tie the ribbon around the wheat, much to the dismay of her sisters. *Baka* Fania would soothe their wounded feelings by handing out candied figs, secretly slipping Alina a sweet, as well.

Her grandmother had loved her so much. She would hate to see Alina so unhappy now, especially if she knew the source of the unhappiness was her own prediction about Alina's future.

Alina loved Eric. She couldn't imagine ever feeling this way about another man, no matter what color hair he had.

Then there was the whole U.S. government to consider. Immigration didn't grant residency permits to just anyone these days. So-called "green-card marriages" were a thing of the past. Now a couple had to prove the seriousness of their relationship and even then it could take months, even years, for the paperwork to wend its way through the proper channels.

Maybe Grandmother, in her wisdom, knew the pain of that trial would be worse than anything Alina endured now.

But Christmas was a time for miracles—from the miracle of sprouting wheat in the dead of winter to unexpected gifts of all sorts. Alina didn't know if finding a way to be with Eric would qualify as a full-blown miracle, but she was willing to send up a prayer to both God and *Baka* Fania that they make it so.

Chapter Thirteen

A few days later, Alina stopped Marissa as she emerged from Mr. Herrerra's room. "How is he doing?" Alina asked.

Marissa shook her head. "No improvement. His doctor started a new treatment this morning."

"And they think that will help?"

"Who knows? He's so fragile right now, things could go either way."

"How is Mrs. Herrera?"

"Poor dear. She's putting up a brave front, but I know she's scared."

"I should go to her."

She started past her friend, but Marissa stopped her. "Not right now. She's napping on the cot we set up for her. She refuses to go home and sleep, so this was the best we could do."

Alina nodded and followed her friend down the hall. "This illness has been as hard on her as it has on Mr. Herrera," she said.

"I guess that's the 'for worse' part of the wedding

vows," Marissa said. "Though if you asked her, I bet she'd say she wouldn't trade a moment of being with him."

Alina sighed. What would it be like to love someone that much, for so long?

"I saw Eric last night," Marissa said.

"Oh." She'd told Marissa she didn't want to talk about Eric, but her friend ignored this request.

"He brought in a woman from Lifeway Manor who'd injured her back."

"Another video game injury?" Hospital staff had started keeping a tally of injured "athletes" from the assisted-living complex.

"You got it. I think she said she was golfing. Anyway, he asked about you."

Alina stiffened.

"He always asks about you," Marissa said. "He's still crazy about you."

And she was crazy about him. On one level it was stupid that they remained apart, but on another it made even more sense for them to keep their distance. She'd been over the arguments for and against their relationship hundreds of times and no clear winner emerged.

"You should come to my house for Christmas dinner," Marissa said, abruptly changing the subject.

Christmas was only a week away. "I signed up to work that day." Better to be here at the hospital than sitting at home alone.

"Come by after your shift, then. You should have a better Christmas dinner than the one you'll have here. My mom's a good cook."

"Maybe I'll do that. Thank you." She planned to call

her parents that morning and open gifts while they were on the phone. In that way they could be a little part of each other's celebrations.

Eric would be celebrating with his family. She imagined them around a huge tree, piles of gifts for all the nieces and nephews, brothers and sisters, aunts and uncles and cousins. Later, they'd gather at the long table, laden with food lovingly prepared by the women.

Would he think of her and the kisses they'd shared at Thanksgiving? She knew she'd think of him as she tied the ribbon around the little sheaf of wheat. Would he remember those stolen moments with the sadness she was sure would ever after taint the holidays for her?

ERIC LIKED HIS WORK with ski patrol and EMS because no two days were the same. Every hour offered the potential for a new challenge. He imagined a medical career would be much the same: some routine but enough variety to keep things interesting.

On this particular day, a week before Christmas, he'd already tended a snowboarder with a broken wrist, helped reunite a lost child with her parents and spent an hour running speed-control duty on one of the more crowded runs. Now he was headed back to the base area for his lunch break, down a black diamond run named Jokerville.

He liked the run for its roller-coaster quality—steep pitches followed by flatter sections. He'd just started down one when a figure in pink and white catapulted past him. Blond hair flying, the skier hit the ground, bounced, then tumbled, cartwheeling down the slope in a fall worthy of endless video replays—if only someone had been around to tape it.

Eric raced to the woman's side, sure he'd be confronted with twisted limbs, broken bones or worse. "Are you all right?" he called.

She wiggled her legs. One ski was still attached, the other jutted from a nearby snowbank. "I'm okay," she said. "Just really, really embarrassed."

Eric clicked out of his skis and stomped through the snow to retrieve her abandoned one, then edged his way over to her. "Does your back feel okay?" he asked. "How's your head?"

"I'm fine, really." She pushed herself into a sitting position and brushed snow from her goggles.

"That was some fall," Eric said. "You'd better take it easy for a minute."

She nodded and looked back up the slope. "This is supposed to be fun, right?"

"It can be a lot of fun," he said. "You were having a great time until you fell, right?"

"I was scared silly," she said. "I don't usually ski runs this steep."

"Once you get past the fear, it can be a great rush." He offered her his hand. "Want to try standing?"

She took his hand and pulled herself to her feet.

"Everything okay?" he asked.

She shook out her arms and legs. "Seems to be."

"You're lucky." He'd seen people take far less spectacular tumbles and end up at Gunnison Valley Hospital awaiting surgery to repair twisted ligaments or broken bones.

"I guess." She brushed snow from her pants and jacket. "So how do you get past the fear?" she asked.

"You just keep pushing your boundaries until things that used to scare you don't anymore."

She looked up the slope again. "Maybe I got a little overly ambitious. My boyfriend skis these runs all the time, and I wanted to be able to go with him."

"Look at it this way. You got a bad fall out of the way and you're okay. From now on, you're golden."

She laughed. "I guess that's one way to look at it." Using him for balance, she clicked into her ski, then planted her poles. "I'm a little shaky, I'll admit."

"I'll ski with you the rest of the way down. We'll take it slow."

They started out at a crawl, the woman making wide sweeps across the slopes, avoiding the fall line. As they progressed, she began to relax, and by the time they reached the smoother terrain near the base, she was skiing with confidence. "You'll probably be stiff tonight," Eric said. "You might want to find a hot tub to soak in, or take a hot bath."

"Thanks." She flashed a bright smile. "And thanks for talking me down."

"You'll do better next time," he said. "Just keep working at it. You'll blow your boyfriend away before you know it."

"I will."

He left her at the ski racks and made his way toward the patrol offices. He hoped the woman did get over her fear. She had the guts and the skills to have a lot of fun.

Too many people let one bad fall or their worries about possible injury keep them from enjoying themselves.

You're one to talk about fear and taking risks came the silent accusation. *You weren't willing to take much of a risk for Alina.*

That truth hurt as much as any bruise or break he'd suffered. He could try to blame Alina or his family or fate or anything else, but in his heart he knew he was the only one at fault for not making things work with Alina.

How many times had he picked up the phone to call her, but what, exactly, was he supposed to say? He couldn't tell her that his mother had decided to welcome her with open arms, or that he had an in with the government that would grant her a new visa. He couldn't pretend that medical school would be a breeze with her by his side, or that together they'd never worry about money or be too busy to spend time together. He couldn't promise her he was really a blonde or that her grandmother had been wrong, or that family and tradition didn't matter in this modern world.

He couldn't lie to her and he couldn't lie to himself. If only he could find a new kind of truth for them both.

At home that evening, Eric found his mother in the kitchen. She had lived half her life in this room, overseeing countless meals for her busy family. While making soup or seasoning beans or chopping vegetables she had offered advice and direction that had guided her children through many a crisis.

"Dinner is almost ready," she said as Eric entered the room. "How was work today?"

"Good. The snow's nice, but it's early season yet, so there aren't a lot of people out. No major accidents."

She nodded. "And you? Are you good, too?"

He pulled a chair out from the kitchen table and sat. "Not so much," he admitted.

"Tell me." The same words she had used over the years to coax from him tales of schoolyard squabbles, failed exams, pretty girls who ignored him and bullies who didn't. Here in this very chair he'd first poured out his dream of becoming a doctor.

"I know you don't want me to go away to medical school this fall," he said.

The hand stirring a pot of soup stilled. "A mother never rests easy when her children are far away," she said.

"I won't be gone forever. I want to come back to Gunnison to practice medicine."

She turned to face him, deep lines furrowing her forehead. "Medical school is so expensive. I wish your father and I could help you more."

"You and Dad have done plenty. Don't worry about the money. I'll get loans and grants and financial aid." He gave her what he hoped was an encouraging smile. "You and Dad raised all of us kids on his salary. You taught me a thing or two about stretching a dollar. I'll be fine."

She managed a tight smile. "It's not only the money. These young doctors work so hard. When I volunteered with the hospital auxiliary I used to see them, dead on their feet."

"I know it won't be easy, but I'm tough. I'll get through it all right."

"Yes, you are always the tough guy. The daredevil."

Her smile crumpled at the corners. "Of all my children, you are the one who has worried me the most. Can you blame me for wanting to see you settled here, with a wife and children to keep you close—to keep you safe."

"Aww, Mama." He stood and pulled her close. When had she shrunk so small? Her head barely reached his shoulders. "Don't cry," he said. "I'll stay safe. And I'll come home, I promise."

She sniffed and pushed away. "Don't mind a silly old woman. You'll be a wonderful doctor. I'm sorry if you thought I didn't believe that." She looked up at him, eyes shining. "And don't think I don't know how you children talk about my matchmaking, but it's only because I want the best for you."

"I know you want me to get married and settle down," he began. "And I want those things, too. But it has to be a woman I choose."

She nodded. "Of course. As long as you choose wisely."

"I love Alina."

She turned back to the pot on the stove and stirred more vigorously. "You say that now, but what about five years from now?" she asked. "Ten years from now? Is she really the woman who will make you happy? When all she knows is so different from all you know?"

"All those outer things don't matter so much. Inside, we're the same." They both cared about helping people. They both had a practical nature others didn't always see. Family was important to both of them.

His mother pursed her lips but said nothing.

"Do you remember when I decided to become a paramedic?" Eric asked. "No one in our family had ever done anything like that before."

"Yes. Though several of my sisters are nurses."

"But then I said I wanted to go to medical school. No one in our family had ever done that."

"Yes. We already talked about that. What does this have to do with Alina?"

"I'm trying to point out that I've done a lot of 'different' things no one else in our family has tried," he said. "And they've all worked out well."

She turned from the stove to face him. "The decision to marry and raise a family with someone is more serious than taking a new job or enrolling in medical school," she said.

He stood. "Is it? They're all decisions that alter the course of a person's life." His voice softened. "You were wrong about medical school. Maybe you're wrong about Alina, too?"

Her expression grew more troubled, but when her eyes met his they were kind. "You really do love her?" she asked.

"Yes."

"And you don't think you can be happy with someone else?"

"No, Mama. I only want Alina."

She hesitated, then said. "She is a sweet girl. And I only want you to be happy."

"Alina will make me happy. You'll see." He kissed her and turned to go.

"Where are you going?" she cried.

"I have some things I need to do. I may be back late. Don't bother waiting up."

THE WHEAT WAS FOUR INCHES HIGH the night Alina hurried down Elk Avenue, hoping she could make it to the store before it closed. Tears kept filling her eyes, blurring her vision, their tracks freezing on her face. She dashed them away and kept walking, head down against the swirling wind that sent snowflakes flying around her as if she was inside a giant snow globe.

A cold snow globe. She wished she'd taken the time to change into jeans and a sweater before leaving Gunnison, but she'd been in such a hurry to complete this errand she'd left directly from work. The thin cotton scrubs she wore beneath her coat did little to insulate her from the rapidly falling temperatures.

She passed the post office and the brightly lit tree out front. The building behind it was adorned with more lights and evergreen wreaths tied with red bows. The music of Christmas carols drifted from a nearby restaurant; the whole scene was straight out of a postcard illustrating the Perfect Small-Town Christmas. The thought sent a fresh flood of tears to her eyes. This time she didn't even bother brushing them away.

Instead, she picked up her pace, practically running the last few yards to Pine Needles. "Please tell me you're not closing," she said to the woman behind the register as she burst through the door.

The young woman looked up from counting a stack of bills. "I can stay open a little longer," she said. "What can I get for you?"

Alina looked around, praying the item she wanted had not already been sold. But the shawl was still there, the soft pink folds light and warm against her skin as she lifted it off the shoulders of the mannequin. "This," she said. "I want this."

The shopkeeper smiled. "For yourself? Or is someone going to have a very nice Christmas gift?"

"It's a gift. For a friend." Alina watched as the young woman wrapped the shawl in folds of tissue. "Thank you," she said as she collected her change and dropped it into her purse. "Thank you so much." Then she was out in the snow again, hurrying back down the street toward the Chamber of Commerce lot where she'd left her car.

"Alina!"

She was crossing the street toward the parking lot when she heard her name. At first she thought she'd imagined the sound, then she saw a familiar figure striding toward her through the swirling snow. "Eric!" she gasped.

"Alina, I've been looking all over for you." He grasped her shoulders and turned her toward him.

She wanted to throw her arms around him, to sob and laugh and rage and give vent to all the conflicting emotions that had battered her for days. But as always common sense took over. She glanced toward the lights of an approaching car. "We'd better get out of the street," she said.

Eric pulled her to the sidewalk, where they stood in the shadow of the lighted evergreen that marked the crossroads. "Marissa told me she thought you were here," he said. "What sent you all the way out here so late?"

"I needed to buy a gift for a friend."

"A friend?"

"A woman at the hospital. Her husband's been so sick…" She swallowed a fresh knot of tears. "Oh, Eric, it's so amazing. He's been so sick and we've been afraid he wouldn't make it, but today he rallied and he's really starting to improve. I think he did it for her—so she wouldn't be alone at Christmas."

"No one should be alone at Christmas," he said, and smoothed his hands down her arms.

"Eric, what are you doing here? Why are you looking for me?"

"I've been thinking," he said. "About you. About us. About how much of a coward I've been."

"You're not a coward!" she protested.

"Not usually, but when it came to my personal life, I have been. At first I avoided getting serious about anyone because I was afraid to change my life. I was afraid of being responsible for someone else, I guess. Then I met you."

She remembered that night, here at this very crossroads. The moment she'd seen him, something had stirred inside of her. Had he felt it, too?

"I knew that you were different from the other women I'd dated," he said. "I knew I was falling in love with you, but still I tried to pretend it was a temporary fling. Even when I realized my feelings went deeper than that, I let fear talk me out of doing anything about it."

"What were you afraid of?" she asked.

"Of disappointing my family. Of making a mistake. I'd made such a big deal out of going to medical school. I was terrified of doing anything to mess that up. I still am."

She nodded. "Doing anything different—going against family tradition—*is* scary. No one in my family has ever tried to go against one of *Baka* Fania's predictions."

"My parents just want me to be happy," he said. "I'm sure your grandmother would have wanted that, too. And all that immigration paperwork—we'll find a way to get through that, too. I'll even come and live in Croatia for a while if I have to. It doesn't matter, as long as we can be together."

"What about medical school?"

"I realized today I've been looking at this the wrong way. I've been thinking of marriage as an extra responsibility, another thing to take care of. I'd forgotten it's a shared responsibility. Instead of fighting all my battles by myself, I could have you with me, sharing the load and giving me something to focus on other than the next test or the next payment." He squeezed her arm. "What do you think?"

She looked down at the pink plastic bag that contained the knit shawl. "I decided tonight that if Mr. Herrera can find a way to get well at Christmas, you and I can find a way to be together."

"Forever," he said.

"Yes. Forever."

They sealed the promise with a kiss. He held her tightly and closed his eyes, but she kept her eyes open, not wanting to miss a moment of the lighted tree and the swirling snow and all the magic of love at Christmas.

Epilogue

"Hold still!" Sofia ordered as she struggled to pin a sprig of rosemary to Eric's lapel.

"Why do I have to wear this again?" he asked. "It makes me smell like a roasting chicken."

"Because it's traditional in her country." She smoothed the jacket lapel and stepped back. "There. You look nice. Not at all like the bratty little boy I remember."

"How's Alina?" he asked. Despite his objections, he'd been kept from her for the past twenty-four hours.

"Nervous. Her mother and sister keep fussing with her dress and the flowers. We'll all feel better once this is over with."

Eric would feel better, too. After a year of flights between Colorado and Croatia, a year in which he'd been accepted to and begun medical school at the University of Colorado and Alina had won a coveted green card, or permit of legal residency, all he wanted was for the woman he loved to legally be his wife.

"You look so handsome!" His mother, dressed in a pale mauve silk sheath, hurried forward, handkerchief in hand. She blotted her eyes. "I can't believe my baby is finally going to be married," she said.

"I told you it would happen," Eric said. "I just had to find the right woman. The one *I* chose."

"I've said all along that Alina is a very sweet girl," Mrs. Sepulveda said. "And I've seen how happy she makes you, so of course I'm glad to welcome her to the family."

"Thank you, Mama." He bent and kissed her cheek. "Are you ready?"

He turned to see Marty, imposing in a dark robe and clerical stole. "I'm ready," Eric said. "I really appreciate you making the trip back to Gunnison to do this." Newly graduated from seminary, Marty had accepted a post in a church in Colorado's San Luis valley.

"Alina insisted," Marty said. "Something about it being what her grandmother would have wanted. I didn't understand that, but I'm honored to do this for you both."

Eric smiled. Alina had decided that if Marty performed their wedding ceremony, her grandmother's prediction would be fulfilled—a big blond man would have provided the key to her happiness.

Organ music sounded from within the sanctuary. "I'd better get back to Alina," Sofia said. She was serving as bridesmaid, with Marissa as the maid of honor. "Mama, it's almost time for you to be seated."

"I know," Mrs. Sepulveda said. "I've done this before. Remember?"

After a last-minute flurry of activity, Eric was alone in the little side room, except for Marty and his brothers John and Bart, who were standing up as his best men.

"Come on then," Marty said, straightening his stole. "Let's do this."

"Let's do it," Eric said.

The next hour was a blur of sensation: the throb of organ music, the scent of flowers, the cadence of old prayers and sacred vows and the image he would remember forever, Alina walking down the aisle in a white lace dress, carrying a bouquet of wheat and roses, smiling for him.

Only for him.

* * *

'THIS EVENING I'm flying to New York for two weeks,'
Jasim imparted with a casualness that made her heart sink
like a stone. 'That's why I had you brought here. I own this
apartment and you'll be comfortable here while I'm abroad.'

'I can afford my own accommodation although I may not
need it for long. I'll have another job by the time you
get back—'

Jasim released a slightly harsh laugh. 'There's no need for
you to look for another position. How would I ever see you?
Don't you understand what I'm offering you?'

Elinor stood very still. 'No, I must be incredibly thick
because I haven't quite worked out yet what you're offering
me.…'

His charismatic smile slashed his lean dark visage.
'Naturally, I want to take care of you.…'

'No, thanks.' Elinor forced a smile and mentally willed him not to demean her with some sordid proposition. 'The only man who will ever take *care* of me with my agreement will be my husband. I'm willing to wait for you to come back but I'm not willing to be kept by you. I'm a very independent woman and what I give, I give freely.'

Jasim frowned. 'You make it all sound so serious.'

'What happened between us last night left pure chaos in its wake. Right now, I don't know whether I'm on my head or my heels. I'll stay for a while because I have nowhere else to go in the short term. So maybe it's good that you'll be away for a while.'

Jasim pulled out his wallet to extract a card. 'My private number,' he told her, presenting her with it as though it was a precious gift, which indeed it was. Many women would have done just about anything to gain access to that direct hotline to him, but his staff guarded his privacy with scrupulous care.

Before he could close the wallet, his blood ran cold in his veins. How could he have made such a serious oversight? What if he had got her pregnant? He knew that an unplanned pregnancy would engulf his life like an avalanche, crush his freedom and suffocate him. He barely stilled a shudder at the threat of such an outcome and thought how ironic it was that what his older brother had longed and prayed for to secure the line to the throne should strike Jasim as an absolute disaster....

* * *

What will proud Prince Jasim do if Elinor is expecting his royal baby? Perhaps an arranged marriage is the only solution! But will Elinor agree? Find out in DESERT PRINCE, BRIDE OF INNOCENCE by Lynne Graham [#2884], available from Harlequin Presents® in January 2010.

HARLEQUIN® *Blaze*™

New Year, New Man!

*For the perfect New Year's punch,
blend the following:*

- *One woman determined to find her inner vixen*
- *A notorious—and notoriously hot!—playboy*
- *A provocative New Year's Eve bash*
- *An impulsive kiss that leads to a night of
explosive passion!*

When the clock hits midnight Claire Daniels
kisses the guy standing closest to her, but
the kiss doesn't end after the bells stop ringing....

Look for

Moonstruck

by *USA TODAY* bestselling author

JULIE KENNER

Available January

red-hot reads

www.eHarlequin.com

HB79518

REQUEST YOUR FREE BOOKS!

2 FREE NOVELS PLUS 2 FREE GIFTS!

HARLEQUIN®

American ★ Romance®

Love, Home & Happiness!

YES! Please send me 2 FREE Harlequin® American Romance® novels and my 2 FREE gifts (gifts are worth about $10). After receiving them, if I don't wish to receive any more books, I can return the shipping statement marked "cancel." If I don't cancel, I will receive 4 brand-new novels every month and be billed just $4.24 per book in the U.S. or $4.99 per book in Canada.* That's a savings of close to 15% off the cover price! It's quite a bargain! Shipping and handling is just 50¢ per book. I understand that accepting the 2 free books and gifts places me under no obligation to buy anything. I can always return a shipment and cancel at any time. Even if I never buy another book from Harlequin, the two free books and gifts are mine to keep forever.

154 HDN E4DS   354 HDN E4D4

Name _____ (PLEASE PRINT) _____

Address _____ Apt. # _____

City _____ State/Prov. _____ Zip/Postal Code _____

Signature (if under 18, a parent or guardian must sign) _____

Mail to the **Harlequin Reader Service:**
IN U.S.A.: P.O. Box 1867, Buffalo, NY 14240-1867
IN CANADA: P.O. Box 609, Fort Erie, Ontario L2A 5X3

Not valid to current subscribers of Harlequin® American Romance® books.

Want to try two free books from another line?
Call 1-800-873-8635 or visit www.morefreebooks.com.

* Terms and prices subject to change without notice. Prices do not include applicable taxes. N.Y. residents add applicable sales tax. Canadian residents will be charged applicable provincial taxes and GST. Offer not valid in Quebec. This offer is limited to one order per household. All orders subject to approval. Credit or debit balances in a customer's account(s) may be offset by any other outstanding balance owed by or to the customer. Please allow 4 to 6 weeks for delivery. Offer available while quantities last.

Your Privacy: Harlequin is committed to protecting your privacy. Our Privacy Policy is available online at www.eHarlequin.com or upon request from the Reader Service. From time to time we make our lists of customers available to reputable third parties who may have a product or service of interest to you. If you would prefer we not share your name and address, please check here. ☐

HAR09R2